THE YOUNG PITCHER

THE YOUNG PITCHER
ZANE GREY

FOREWORD BY
JOHN THORN

BEECH TREE BOOKS
NEW YORK

Printed in the United States of America.

First Beech Tree Edition, 1992.

1   2   3   4   5   6   7   8   9   10

Library of Congress Cataloging-in-Publication Data
Grey, Zane, 1872–1939.
The young pitcher/by Zane Grey : foreword by John Thorn.
p.   cm.
Originally published : New York : Harper & Brothers, 1911.
Summary: As a new freshman at Wayne College, Ken Ward finds a way
to win recognition through his pitching skills on the newly-formed
baseball team.
ISBN 0-688-11262-5
[1. Baseball—Fiction.   2. Universities and colleges—Fiction.]
I. Title.
PZ7.G875Yo   1992
[Fic]—dc20   91-23670 CIP AC

CONTENTS

FOREWORD

Zane Grey (1872–1939) was a fabulously successful writer; his 85 books sold more than 100 million copies and inspired 111 films, all of them Westerns. But the road to fame as America's Man of the West was a long and circuitous one, and Grey's flurry of baseball writing in 1909–1911, based on his personal experiences in the East, stands as an interesting milepost.

Pearl Zane Gray (the name he was born with, and didn't change until his twenties) grew up in Zanesville, Ohio, a dentist's son who found school confining. Fishing and woodsmanship and baseball were his life. When he was eighteen, the family moved to the state's capital, Columbus, where his pitching skills caught the attention of a scout for the University of Pennsylvania. Enrolling there at the rather advanced age of twenty, Grey struggled through four years to earn his degree in dentistry, distinguishing himself far more on the varsity ball field than in class. He played baseball professionally for four years after graduation and as a semipro until 1902.

At the age of thirty, dispirited about his lack of success as a dentist, he determined to become a writer. His not yet fertile imagination produced *Betty Zane*, a historical potboiler about his great-great-aunt that no commercial publisher would touch; he borrowed money to have it printed and in 1903 issued it himself. A sequel to this book, featuring one of the subordinate characters, appeared in 1906 (*The Spirit of the Border*).

His ball playing and his dentistry were over; his writing career seemed stillborn; he was broke; and despite his boyhood passion for outdoor sport, he had never been west of Ohio. Yet only six years later he was nationally famous as a roper of mountain lions, an ardent conservationist, and the author of *Riders of the Purple Sage*, his most enduring novel. What brought about this transformation? His realization, after a 1907 expedition to the Grand Canyon with Charles J. "Buffalo" Jones, that to tell a compelling story he had to ground it in personal experience. After a second trip to Arizona with the great animal protectionist, Grey wrote *The Last of the Plainsmen*. Its modest success encouraged him to try, in 1909, a baseball novel that was based on his boyhood involvement in the game he loved: *The Shortstop*, which Morrow has reissued as a companion volume to the book you hold in your hands.

The Shortstop proved a hit, inspiring Grey to embark upon a series of juvenile books, each based on personal experience, featuring hero Ken Ward. The first of these was *The Young Forester* (1910), in which Grey denounced not only the wanton deforestation by the huge timber companies but also their misguided efforts toward reforestation. The second, published in 1911, was *The Young Pitcher;* in it, Grey tackled one of the larger issues of his day (and ours)—the relationship between athletics and academics. *The Young Lion Hunter* was also issued in 1911, thus recapitulating in the four novels his life to the point of his pivotal trips with Buffalo Jones.

FOREWORD

Before completing the juvenile cycle with *Ken Ward in the Jungle* and publishing *Riders of the Purple Sage*, both in 1912, Grey wrote a number of baseball stories for various magazines, which years later were collected in *The Redheaded Outfield and Other Stories*. Why did Grey write so much about baseball during his formative years as a writer, and never again thereafter? Because the game was emblematic of a boy's progress toward manhood (and in Grey's case, the profound need to incorporate the spirit of adventure into the pursuit of a career) and because he knew baseball as no other major American novelist has.

Mark Twain built a baseball scene into *A Connecticut Yankee in King Arthur's Court*; Thomas Wolfe recalled his boyhood memories of the game in sections of *You Can't Go Home Again*; Bernard Malamud, Philip Roth, and W. P. Kinsella set entire novels in the land of baseball. But in their youth, none of these authors played the game with such intensity and skill that they rose from the sandlots to stardom, in both the collegiate and professional ranks. Zane Grey did.

As a boy Grey's only equal on the local diamond was younger brother Romer, or "Reddy," who went on to a notable career as a minor-league outfielder and even played one game in 1903 with the Pittsburgh Pirates. The redheaded Romer is fictionalized as Reddy Ray in *The Young Pitcher* and in the story "The Redheaded Outfield."

At the University of Pennsylvania, Zane Grey came under the tutelage of Arthur "Sandy" Irwin, fictionalized as Manager MacSandy in *The Shortstop* and, in *The Young Pitcher*, as Worry Arthurs. Irwin was a star shortstop for several major-league teams in the 1880s and managed for eight years.

FOREWORD

Grey shifted from the pitcher's box to the outfield in 1893, his sophomore year, when the new distance to home plate of sixty feet, six inches straightened his curveball. During his four years of varsity ball, his many exploits included a great catch at New York's Polo Grounds to help Penn defeat the New York Giants in a spring exhibition contest and a two-out, two-run homer in the ninth inning to vanquish the University of Virginia. Especially memorable for Grey was a bit of freshman hazing that culminated in his fighting off a band of sophomores by hurling potatoes at them, an incident that is recounted in the second chapter of *The Young Pitcher*. In real life, the event led Penn's Art Irwin to take note of Grey's great arm; in this book, Ken Ward's way with a spud moves Wayne University's Worry Arthurs to place the freshman on the varsity team.

In an interesting latter-day sidelight, all eyes were on the potato's return to baseball in 1987, when Williamsport's Dave Bresnahan used one to pull a hidden-ball trick in a game with Eastern League rival Reading. Before the game, Bresnahan (a catcher like his great-uncle, Hall of Famer Roger Bresnahan) carved a potato to resemble a baseball and hid it on his person. With a Reading runner on third base, Bresnahan deliberately threw the potato into left field, in a seemingly botched pickoff attempt. The runner trotted home, only to find the catcher waiting for him, baseball in hand. The club directors of Williamsport were not amused: they released Bresnahan the next day.

Grey went on to play professional ball for Wheeling in the Iron and Oil League of 1895 under a false name to maintain his college eligibility for 1896. This maneuver was so common at the time that even a player as prominent as Eddie Collins, a Hall of Fame second baseman, began his career with the Philadelphia A's as a moon-lighting collegian, playing under the name of Sullivan. Over the next four years Grey played in such minor leagues as the Interstate, the Atlantic, and the Eastern. Even after setting up his dentistry practice in New York City in 1899, Grey continued to play on weekends for the powerhouse Orange Athletic Club of Orange, New Jersey, a semipro outfit that played Sunday exhibitions against big-league clubs and frequently defeated them.

Important as Grey's baseball days were to him personally and crucial though his baseball writing was to the advance of his craft, why would anyone want to read a book like *The Young Pitcher* today? It is a conventional tale, conventionally told in the pluck-and-luck format of the Horatio Alger and Frank Merriwell series. The novel's prose style may have its detractors, but what commands *The Young Pitcher* to our attention is that it does bear the hallmark of a Zane Grey book: it tells a good story. It also offers a fascinating glimpse of how different the old game of baseball was, with its reliance upon the bunt and choked-bat hitting, its now-strange rules variations, and its wide-eyed wonder at such commonplace mysteries as the curveball.

In addition, the novel provides a rich and atmospheric backdrop of university life at the turn of the century, not so much different from that of today in its class warfare, neo-tribal rituals, and obsession with sport. It is difficult, for example, to read President Halstead's stirring speech to the undergraduates ("Sport is too much with us") and not think of today's campus athletic problems and occa-sional scandals. The "taint of professionalism" that dis-turbs President Halstead remains, nearly a century later, the central issue of the top-rank university sports programs.

Grey is clearly in accord with Halstead's views. But for him, baseball was the principal attraction of college life, so his voice can also be heard in one of Worry Arthurs's concluding sentiments: "Sure, it was only baseball, but, after all, I think good, hard play, on the square and against long odds, will do as much for you as your studies." A university education may prepare one for a career, Grey believed, but it was in the struggle to overcome adversity—baseball as the proverbial school of hard knocks—that one gained an education for life.

That was the story of his own twisty path to success, as Grey came to see it. His years at Penn, and the baseball writing that followed, were crucial to his development as a writer and as a man. This gives *The Young Pitcher* an added dimension that makes its reissue, exactly 100 years after Grey's freshman year, most welcome.

JOHN THORN

·1·

THE VARSITY CAPTAIN

KEN WARD had not been at the big university many days before he realized the miserable lot of a freshman.

At first he was sorely puzzled. College was so different from what he had expected. At the high school of his hometown, which, being the capital of the state, was no village, he had been somebody. Then his summer in Arizona, with its wild adventures, had given him a self-appreciation which made his present situation humiliating.

There were more than four thousand students at the university. Ken felt himself the youngest, the smallest, the one of least consequence. He was lost in a shuffle of superior youths. In the forestry department he was a mere boy; and he soon realized that a freshman there was the same as anywhere. The fact that he weighed nearly one hundred and sixty pounds, and was no stripling, despite his youth, made not one whit of difference.

Unfortunately, his first overture of what he con-

1

sidered good-fellowship had been made to an up-
perclassman and had been a grievous mistake.
Ken had not yet recovered from its reception. He
grew careful after that, then shy, and finally began
to struggle against disappointment and loneliness.

Outside of his department, on the campus and
everywhere he ventured, he found things still
worse. There was something wrong with him,
with his fresh complexion, with his hair, with the
way he wore his tie, with the cut of his clothes.
In fact, there was nothing right about him. He
had been so beset that he could not think of anything but himself. One day, while sauntering
along a campus path, with his hands in his pockets, he met two students coming toward him.
They went to the right and left, and, jerking his
hands from his pockets, roared in each ear, "How
dare you walk with your hands in your pockets!"

Another day, on the library steps, he encoun-
tered a handsome bareheaded youth with a fine,
clean-cut face and keen eyes, who showed the
true stamp of the great university.

"Here," he said, sharply, "aren't you a freshman?"

"Why—yes," confessed Ken.

"I see you have your trousers turned up at the
bottom."

"Yes—so I have." For the life of him Ken could
not understand why that simple fact seemed a
crime, but so it was.

"Turn them down!" ordered the student.

Ken looked into the stern face and flashing eyes of his tormentor, and then meekly did as he had been commanded.

"Boy, I've saved your life. We murder freshmen here for that," said the student, and then passed on up the steps.

In the beginning it was such incidents as these that had bewildered Ken. He passed from surprise to anger, and vowed he would have something to say to these upperclassmen. But when the opportunity came Ken always felt so little and mean that he could not retaliate. This made him furious. He had not been in college two weeks before he could distinguish the sophomores from the seniors by the look on their faces. He hated the sneering "Sophs," and felt rising in him the desire to fight. But he both feared and admired seniors. They seemed so aloof, so far above him. He was in awe of them and had a hopeless longing to be like them. And as for the freshmen, it took no second glance for Ken to pick them out. They were of two kinds—those who banded together in crowds and went about yelling, and running away from the Sophs, and those who sneaked about alone with timid step and furtive glance.

Ken was one of these lonesome freshmen. He was pining for companionship, but he was afraid to open his lips. Once he had dared to go into Carlton Hall, the magnificent clubhouse which had been given to the university by a famous graduate. The club was for all students—Ken had read that on the card sent to him, and also in the papers. But manifestly the upperclassmen had a different point of view. Ken had gotten a glimpse into the immense reading room with its open fire-place and huge chairs, its air of quiet study and repose; he had peeped into the brilliant billiard hall and the gymnasium; and he had been so impressed and delighted with the marble swimming tank that he had forgotten himself and walked too near the pool. Several students accidentally bumped him into it. It appeared the students were so eager to help him out that they crowded him in again. When Ken finally got out he learned the remarkable fact that he was the sixteenth fresh-man who had been accidentally pushed into the tank that day.

So Ken Ward was in a state of revolt. He was homesick; he was lonely for a friend; he was constantly on the lookout for some trick; his confidence in himself had fled; his opinion of himself had suffered a damaging change; he hardly dared call his soul his own.

But that part of his time spent in study or attending lectures more than made up for the other. Ken loved his subject and was eager to learn. He had a free hour in the afternoon, and often he passed this in the library, sometimes in the different exhibition halls. He wanted to go into Carlton Hall again, but his experience there made him refrain.

One afternoon at this hour Ken happened to glance into a lecture room. It was a large amphitheater full of noisy students. The benches were arranged in a circle running up from a small pit. Seeing safety in the number of students who were passing in, Ken went along. He thought he might hear an interesting lecture. It did not occur to him that he did not belong there. The university had many departments and he felt that any lecture room was open to him. Still, caution had become a habit with him, and he stepped down the steep aisle looking for an empty bench.

How steep the aisle was! The benches appeared to be on the side of a hill. Ken slipped into an empty one. There was something warm and pleasant in the close contact of so many students, in the ripple of laughter and the murmur of voices. Ken looked about him with a feeling that he was glad to be there.

It struck him, suddenly, that the room had grown strangely silent. Even the shuffling steps of the incoming students had ceased. Ken gazed upward with a queer sense of foreboding. Perhaps he only imagined that all the students above were looking down at him. Hurriedly he glanced below. A sea of faces, in circular rows, was turned his way.

There was no mistake about it. He was the

attraction. At the same instant when he prayed to sink through the bench out of sight a burning anger filled his breast. What on earth had he done now? He knew it was something; he felt it. That quiet moment seemed an age. Then the waiting silence burst.

"*Fresh on fifth!*" yelled a student in one of the lower benches.

"FRESH ON FIFTH!" bawled another at the top of his lungs.

Ken's muddled brain could make little of the matter. He saw he was in the fifth row of benches, and that all the way around on either side of him the row was empty. The four lower rows were packed, and above him students were scattered all over. He had the fifth row of benches to himself.

"Fresh on fifth!"

Again the call rang up from below. It was repeated, now from the left of the pit and then from the right. A student yelled it from the first row and another from the fourth. It banged back and forth. Not a word came from the upper part of the room.

Ken sat up straight with a very red face. It was his intention to leave the bench, but embarrassment that was developing into resentment held him fast. What a senseless lot these students were! Why could they not leave him in peace? How foolish of him to go wandering about in strange lecture rooms!

A hand pressed Ken's shoulder. He looked back to see a student bending down toward him.

"*Hang, Freshie!*" this fellow whispered.

"What's it all about?" asked Ken. "What have I done, anyway? I never was in here before."

"All Sophs down there. They don't allow freshmen to go below the sixth row. There've been several rushes this term. And the big one's coming. Hang, Freshie! We're all with you."

"Fresh on fifth!" The tenor of the cry had subtly changed. Good-humored warning had changed to challenge. It pealed up from many lusty throats and became general all along the four packed rows.

"*Hang, Freshie!*" bellowed a freshman from the topmost row. It was acceptance of the challenge, the battle cry flung down to the Sophs. A roar arose from the pit. The freshmen, outnumbering the sophomores, drowned the roar in a hoarser one. Then both sides settled back in ominous waiting.

Ken thrilled in all his being. The freshmen were with him! That roar told him of united strength. All in a moment he had found comrades, and he clenched his fingers into the bench, vowing he would hang there until hauled away.

"Fresh on fifth!" shouted a Soph in ringing

voice. He stood up in the pit and stepped to the back of the second bench. "Fresh on fifth! Watch me throw him out!"

He was a sturdily built young fellow and balanced himself gracefully on the backs of the benches, stepping up from one to the other. There was a bold gleam in his eyes and a smile on his face. He showed good-natured contempt for a freshman and an assurance that was close to authority.

Ken sat glued to his seat in mingled fear and wrath. Was he to be the butt of those overbearing sophomores? He thought he could do nothing but hang on with all his might. The ascending student jumped upon the fourth bench and, reaching up, laid hold of Ken with no gentle hands. His grip was so hard that Ken had difficulty in stifling a cry of pain. This, however, served to dispel his panic and make him angry clear through.

The sophomore pulled and tugged with all his strength, yet he could not dislodge Ken. The freshmen howled gleefully for him to "Hang! hang!"

Then two more sophomores leaped up to help the leader. A blank silence followed this move, and all the freshmen leaned forward breathlessly. There was a sharp ripping of cloth. Half of Ken's coat appeared in the hands of one of his assailants.

Suddenly Ken let go his hold, pushed one fellow violently, then swung his fists. It might have been unfair, for the sophomores were beneath him and balancing themselves on the steep benches, but Ken was too angry to think of that. The fellow he pushed fell into the arms of the students below, the second slid out of sight, and the third, who had started the fray, plunged with a crash into the pit.

The freshmen greeted this with a wild yell; the sophomores answered likewise. Like climbing, tumbling apes the two classes spilled themselves up and down the benches, and those nearest Ken laid hold of him, pulling him in opposite directions.

Then began a fierce fight for possession of luckless Ken. Both sides were linked together by gripping hands. Ken was absolutely powerless. His clothes were torn to tatters in a twinkling; they were soon torn completely off, leaving only his shoes and socks. Not only was he in danger of being seriously injured, but students of both sides were handled as fiercely. A heavy trampling roar shook the amphitheater. As they surged up and down the steep room benches were split. In the beginning the sophomores had the advantage and the tug-of-war raged near the pit and all about it. But the superior numbers of the freshmen began to tell. The web of close-locked bodies slowly mounted up the room, smashing the benches, swaying downward now and then, yet irresistibly gaining ground. The yells of the freshmen increased with the assurance of victory. There was one more prolonged, straining struggle; then Ken was pulled away from the sophomores. The wide, swinging doors of the room were knocked flat to let out the stream of wild freshmen. They howled like fiends; it was first blood for the freshman class; the first tug won that year.

Ken Ward came to his senses out in the corridor surrounded by an excited, beaming, and disreputable crowd of freshmen. Badly as he was hurt, he had to laugh. Some of them looked happy in nothing but torn underclothes. Others resembled a lot of ragamuffins. Coats were minus sleeves, vests were split, shirts were collarless. Blood and bruises were much in evidence.

Someone helped Ken into a long ulster.

"Say, it was great," said this worthy. "Do you know who that fellow was—the first one who tried to throw you out of number five?"

"I haven't any idea," replied Ken. In fact, he felt that his ideas were as scarce just then as his clothes.

"That was the president of the Sophs. He's the varsity baseball captain, too. You slugged him! . . . Great!"

Ken's spirit, low as it was, sank still lower. What miserable luck he had! His one great ambition, next to getting his diploma, had been to make the varsity baseball team.

· 2 ·

A GREAT ARM

THE SHOCK of that battle, more than the bruising he had received, confined Ken to his room for a week. When he emerged it was to find he was a marked man; marked by the freshmen with a great and friendly distinction, by the sophomores for revenge. If it had not been for the loss of his baseball hopes, he would have welcomed the chance to become popular with his classmates. But for him it was not pleasant to be reminded that he had "slugged" the Sophs' most honored member.

It took only two or three meetings with the revengeful sophomores to teach Ken that discretion was the better part of valor. He learned that the sophomores of all departments were looking for him with deadly intent. So far luck had enabled him to escape all but a wordy bullying. Ken became an expert at dodging. He gave the corridors and campus a wide berth. He relinquished his desire to live in one of the dormitories and rented a room out in the city. He timed his arrival at the university and his departure. His movements were governed entirely by painfully acquired knowledge of the whereabouts of his enemies.

So for weeks Ken Ward lived like a recluse. He was not one with his college mates. He felt that he was not the only freshman who had gotten a bad start in college. Sometimes when he sat near a sad-faced classmate, he knew instinctively that here was a fellow equally in need of friendship. Still these freshmen were as backward as he was, and nothing ever came of such feelings.

The days flew by and the weeks made months, and all Ken did was attend lectures and study. He read everything he could find in the library that had any bearing on forestry. He mastered his textbooks before the Christmas holidays. About the vacation he had long been undecided; at length he made up his mind not to go home. It was a hard decision to reach. But his college life so far had been a disappointment; he was bitter about it, and he did not want his father to know. Judge Ward was a graduate of the university. Often and long he had talked to Ken about university life, the lasting benefit of associations and friendships. He would probably think that his son had barred himself out by some reckless or foolish act. Ken was not sure what was to blame; he knew he had fallen in his own estimation, and that the less he thought of himself the more he hated the Sophs.

On Christmas day he went to Carlton Hall. It was a chance he did not want to miss, for very few students would be there. As it turned out he spent some pleasant hours. But before he left the club his steps led him into the athletic trophy room, and there he was plunged into grief. The place was all ablaze with flags and pennants, silver cups and gold medals, pictures of teams and individuals. There were mounted sculls and oars, footballs and baseballs. The long and proud record of the university was there to be read. All her famous athletes were pictured there, and everyone who had fought for his college. Ken realized that here for the first time he was in the atmosphere of college spirit for which the university was famed. What would he not have given for a permanent place in that gallery! But it was too late. He had humiliated the captain of the baseball team. Ken sought out the picture of the last season's varsity. What a stocky lot of young chaps, all consciously proud of the big letter on their shirts! Dale, the captain and pitcher, was in the center of the group. Ken knew his record, and it was a splendid one. Ken took another look at Dale, another at the famous trainer, Murray, and the professional coach, Arthurs—men under whom it had been his dream to play—and then he left the room, broken-hearted.

When the Christmas recess was over he went back to his lectures resigned to the thought that the athletic side of college life was not for him. He studied harder than ever, and even planned to take a course of lectures in another department. Also his adeptness in dodging was called upon more and more. The Sophs were bound to get him sooner or later. But he did not grow resigned to that; every dodge and flight increased his resentment. Presently he knew he would stop and take what they had to give, and retaliate as best he could. Only, what would they do to him when they did catch him? He remembered his watch, his money, and clothes, never recovered after that memorable tug-of-war. He minded the loss of his watch most; that gift could never be replaced. It seemed to him that he had been the greater sufferer.

One Saturday in January Ken hurried from his classroom. He was always in a hurry and particularly on Saturdays, for that being a short day for most of the departments, there were usually many students passing to and fro. A runaway team clattering down the avenue distracted him from his usual caution, and he cut across the campus. Someone stopped the horses, and a crowd collected. When Ken got there many students were turning away. Ken came face to face with a tall, bronze-haired, freckle-faced sophomore, whom he had dodged more than once. There was now no use in dodging; he had to run or stand his ground.

"Boys, here's that slugging Freshie!" yelled the Soph. "We've got him now."

He might have been an Indian chief, so wild was the whoop that answered him.

"Lead us to him!"

"Oh, what we won't do to that Freshie!"

"Come on, boys!"

Ken heard these yells, saw a number of boys dash at him, then he broke and ran as if for his life. The Sophs, a dozen strong, yelling loudly, strung out after him. Ken headed across the campus. He was fleet of foot, and gained on his pursuers. But the yells brought more Sophs on the scene, and they turned Ken to the right. He spurted for Carlton Hall, and almost ran into the arms of still more sophomores. Turning tail, he fled toward the library. When he looked back it was to see the bronze-haired leader within a hundred yards, and back of him a long line of shouting students.

If there was a place to hide around that library, Ken could not find it. In this circuit he lost ground. Moreover, he discovered he had not used good judgment in choosing that direction. All along the campus was a high iron fence. Ken thought desperately hard for an instant, then with renewed speed he bounded straight for College Hall.

This was the stronghold of the sophomores. As Ken sped up the gravel walk his pursuers split their throats.

"Run, you Freshie!" yelled one.

"The more you run—" yelled another.

"The more we'll skin you!" finished a third.

Ken ran into the passageway leading through College Hall.

It was full of Sophs hurrying toward the door to see where the yells came from. When Ken plunged into their midst someone recognized him and burst out with the information. At the same moment Ken's pursuers banged through the swinging doors.

A yell arose then in the constricted passageway that seemed to Ken to raise College Hall from its foundation. It terrified him. Like an eel he slipped through reaching arms and darted forward. Ken was heavy and fast on his feet, and with fear lending him wings he made a run through College Hall that would have been a delight to the football coach. For Ken was not dodging any sophomores now. He had played his humiliating part of dodger long enough. He knocked them right and left, and many a surprised Soph he tumbled over. Reaching the farther door, he went through out into the open.

The path before him was clear now, and he made straight for the avenue. It was several hundred yards distant, and he got a good start toward it before the Sophs rolled like a roaring stream from the passage. Ken saw other students running, and also men and boys out on the avenue; but as they could not head him off he kept to his course. On that side of the campus a high, narrow stairway, lined by railings, led up to the sidewalk. When Ken reached it he found the steps covered with ice. He slipped and fell three times in the ascent, while his frantic pursuers gained rapidly.

Ken mounted to the sidewalk, gave vent to a gasp of relief, and, wheeling sharply, he stumbled over two boys carrying a bushel basket of potatoes. When he saw the large, round potatoes a daring inspiration flashed into his mind. Taking the basket from the boys he turned to the head of the stairway.

The bronze-haired Soph was halfway up the steps. His followers, twelve or more, were climbing after him. Then a line of others stretched all the way to College Hall.

With a grim certainty of his mastery of the situation Ken threw a huge potato at his leading pursuer. Fair and square on the bronze head it struck with a sharp crack. Like a tenpin the Soph went down. He plumped into the next two fellows, knocking them off their slippery footing. The three fell helplessly and piled up their comrades in a dense wedge halfway down the steps. If the Sophs had been yelling before, it was strange to note how they were yelling now.

Deliberately Ken fired the heavy missiles. They

struck with sodden thuds against the bodies of the struggling sophomores. A poor thrower could not very well have missed that mark, and Ken Ward was remarkably accurate. He had a powerful over-hand swing, and the potatoes flew like bullets. One wild-eyed Soph slipped out of the tangle to leap up the steps. Ken, throwing rather low, hit him on the shin. He buckled and dropped down with a blood-curdling yell. Another shook himself loose and faced upward. A better-aimed shot took him in the shoulder. He gave an exhibition of a high and lofty somersault. Then two more started up abreast. The first Ken hit over the eye with a very small potato, which popped like an explosive bullet and flew into bits. As far as effect was con-cerned a Martini could not have caused a more beautiful fall. Ken landed on the second fellow in the pit of the stomach with a very large potato. There was a sound as of a suddenly struck bass drum. The Soph crumpled up over the railing, slid down, and fell among his comrades, effec-tually blocking the stairway.

For the moment Ken had stopped the advance. The sophomores had been checked by one wild freshman. There was scarcely any doubt about Ken's wildness. He had lost his hat; his disheveled hair stood up like a mane; every time he hurled a potato he yelled. But there was nothing wild about his aim.

All at once he turned his battery on the students

gathering below the crush, trying to find a way through the kicking, slipping mass on the narrow stairs. He scattered them as if they had been quail. Some ran out of range. Others dove for cover and tried to dodge. This dodging brought gleeful howls from Ken.

"Dodge, you Indian!" yelled Ken, as he threw. And seldom it was that dodging was of any use. Then, coming to the end of his ammunition, he surveyed the battlefield beneath him and, turning, ran across the avenue and down a street. At the corner of the block he looked back. There was one man coming, but he did not look like a student. So Ken slackened his pace and bent his steps toward his boardinghouse.

"By George! I stole those potatoes!" he exclaimed presently. "I wonder how I can make that good."

Several times as he turned to look over his shoulder he saw the man he had noticed at first. But that did not trouble him, for he was sure no one else was following him. Ken reached his room, exhausted by exertion and excitement. He flung himself upon his bed to rest and calm his mind so that he could think. If he had been in a bad light before, what was his position now? Beyond all reasoning with, however, was the spirit that gloried in his last stand.

"By George!" he kept saying. "I wouldn't have missed that—not for anything. They made my life a nightmare. I'll have to leave college—go some-where else—but I don't care."

Later, after dinner as he sat reading, he heard a doorbell ring, a man's voice, then footsteps in the hall. Someone tapped on his door. Ken felt a strange, cold sensation, which soon passed, and he spoke:

"Come in."

The door opened to admit a short man with little, bright eyes sharp as knives.

"Hello, Kid," he said. Then he leisurely removed his hat and overcoat and laid them on the bed.

Ken's fear of he knew not what changed to amazement. At least his visitor did not belong to the faculty. There was something familiar about the man, yet Ken could not place him.

"Well up in your studies?" he asked cordially. Then he seated himself, put a hand on each knee, and deliberately and curiously studied Ken.

"Why, yes, pretty well up," replied Ken. He did not know how to take the man. There was a kindliness about him which relieved Ken, yet there was also a hard scrutiny that was embarrassing.

"All by your lonely here," he said.

"It is lonely," replied Ken, "but—but I don't get on very well with the students."

"Small wonder. Most of 'em are crazy."

He was unmistakably friendly. Ken kept wondering where he had seen him. Presently the man arose, and, with a wide smile on his face, reached over and grasped Ken's right arm.

"How's the whip?"

"What?" asked Ken.

"The wing—your arm, Kid, your arm."

"Oh— Why, it's all right."

"It's not sore—not after peggin' a bushel of potatoes on a cold day?"

Ken laughed and raised his arm up and down. "It's weak tonight, but not sore."

"These boys with their India-rubber arms! It's youth, Kid, it's youth. Say, how old are you?"

"Sixteen."

"What! No more than that?"

"No."

"How much do you weigh?"

"About one hundred and fifty-six."

"I thought you had some beef back of that stunt of yours today. Say, Kid, it was the funniest and the best thing I've seen at the university in ten years—and I've seen some fresh boys do some stunts, I have. Well . . . Kid, you've a grand whip—a great arm—and we're goin' to do some stunts with it."

Ken felt something keen and significant in the very air.

"A great arm! For what? . . . who are you?"

"Say, I thought every boy in college knew me. I'm Arthurs."

"The baseball coach! Are you the baseball coach?" exclaimed Ken, jumping up with his heart in his throat.

"That's me, my boy; and I'm lookin' you up."

Ken suddenly choked with thronging emotions and sat down as limp as a rag.

"Yes, Kid, I'm after you strong. The way you pegged 'em today got me. You've a great arm!"

· 3 ·

PRISONER OF THE SOPHS

"BUT if—it's really true—that I've a great arm," faltered Ken, "it won't ever do me any good. I could never get on the varsity."

"Why not?" demanded the coach. "I'll make a star of a youngster like you, if you'll take coachin'. Why not?"

"Oh, you don't know," returned Ken, with a long face.

"Say, you haven't struck me as a kid with no nerve. What's wrong with you?"

"It was I who slugged Captain Dale and caused that big rush between the freshmen and sophomores. I've lived like a hermit ever since."

"So it was you who hit Dale. Well—that's bad," replied Arthurs. He got up with sober face and began to walk the floor. "I remember the eye he had. It was a sight. . . . But Dale's a good fellow. He'll—"

"I'd do anything on earth to make up for that," burst out Ken.

"Good! I'll tell you what we'll do," said Arthurs,

his face brightening. "We'll go right down to Dale's room now. I'll fix it up with him somehow. The sooner the better. I'm goin' to call the baseball candidates to the cage soon."

They put on coats and hats and went out. Evidently the coach was thinking hard, for he had nothing to say, but he kept a reassuring hand on Ken's arm. They crossed the campus along the very path where Ken had fled from the sophomores. The great circle of dormitories loomed up beyond with lights shining in many windows. Arthurs led Ken through a courtyard and into a wide, bright hallway. Their steps sounded with hollow clicks upon the tiled floor. They climbed three fights of stairs, and then Arthurs knocked at a door. Ken's heart palpitated. It was all so sudden; he did not know what he was going to say or do. He did not care what happened to him if Arthurs could only, somehow, put him right with the captain.

A merry voice bade them enter. The coach opened the door and led Ken across the threshold. Ken felt the glow of a warm, bright room, colorful with pennants and posters, and cozy in its disorder. Then he saw Dale and, behind him, several other students. There was a moment's silence in which Ken heard his heart beat.

Dale rose slowly from his seat, the look on his frank face changing from welcome to intense amazement and then wild elation.

"Whoop!" he shouted. "Lock the door! Worry Arthurs, this's your best bet ever!"

Dale dashed at the coach, hugged him frantically, then put his head out of the door to bawl: "Sophs! Sophs! Sophs! Hurry call! Number nine! . . . Oh, my!"

Then he faced about, holding the door partially open. He positively beamed upon the coach.

"Say, Cap, what's eatin' you?" asked Arthurs. He looked dumbfounded. Ken hung to him desperately; he thought he knew what was coming. There were hurried footsteps in the corridor and excited voices.

"Worry, you've got a lot of nerve to bring this freshman here," declared the captain.

"Well, what of it?" demanded the coach. "I looked him up tonight. He's got a great arm, and will be good material for the team. He told me about the little scrap you had in the lecture room. He lost his temper, and no wonder. Anyway, he's sorry, Cap, and I fetched him around to see if you couldn't make it up. How about it, Kid?"

"I'm sorry—awfully sorry, Captain Dale," blurted out Ken. "I was mad and scared, too—then you fellows hurt me. So I hit right out. . . . But I'll take my medicine."

"So—oh!" ejaculated Dale. "Well, this beats the deuce! *That's* why you're here?"

The door opened wide to admit half a dozen eager-faced youths.

"Fellows, here's a surprise," said Dale. "Young Ward, the freshman! the elusive slugging freshman, fast on his feet, and, as Worry here says, a lad with a great arm!"

"WARD!" roared the Sophs in unison.

"Hold on, fellows—wait—no roughhouse yet—wait," ordered Dale. "Ward's here of his own free will!"

Silence ensued after the captain spoke.

While he turned to lock the door the Sophs stared openmouthed at Ken. Arthurs had a worried look, and he kept his hand on Ken. Dale went to a table and began filling his pipe. Then he fixed sharp, thoughtful eyes upon his visitors.

"Worry, you say you brought this freshman here to talk baseball?" he asked.

"Sure I did," blustered Arthurs. It was plain now where he got the name that Dale called him. "What's in the wind, anyhow?"

Dale then gravely spoke to Ken. "So you came here to see me? Sorry you slugged me once? Want to make up for it somehow, because you think you've a chance for the team, and don't want me to be sore on you? That it?"

"Not exactly," replied Ken. "I'd want to let you get square with me even if you weren't the varsity captain."

"Well, you've more than squared yourself with me—by coming here. You'll realize that presently. But don't you know what's happened, what the freshmen have done?"

"No, I don't."

"You haven't been near the university since this afternoon when you pulled off the potato stunt?"

"I should say I haven't."

This brought a laugh from the Sophs.

"You were pretty wise," went on Dale. "The Sophs didn't love you then. But they're going to— understand?"

Ken shook his head, too bewildered and mystified to reply.

"Well now, here's Giraffe Boswick. Look what you did to him!"

Ken's glance followed the wave of Dale's hand and took in the tall, bronze-haired sophomore who had led the chase that afternoon. Boswick wore a huge discolored bruise over his left eye. It was hideous. Ken was further sickened to recollect that Boswick was one of the varsity pitchers. But the fellow was smiling amiably at Ken, as amiably as one eye would permit. The plot thickened about Ken. He felt his legs trembling under him.

"Boswick, you forgive Ward, don't you—now?" continued Dale, with a smile.

"With all my heart!" exclaimed the pitcher. "To see him here would make me forgive anything."

Coach Arthurs was ill at ease. He evidently knew students, and he did not relish the mystery, the hidden meaning.

"Say, you wise guys make me sick," he called out gruffly. "Here's a kid that comes right among you. He's on the level, and more'n that, he's game! Now, Cap, I fetched him here, and I won't stand for a whole lot. Get up on your toes! Get it over!"

"Sit down, Worry, here's a cigar—light up," said Dale, soothingly. "It's all coming right, lovely, I say. Ward was game to hunt me up, a thousand times gamer than he knows. . . . See here, Ward, where are you from?"

"I live a good long day's travel from the university," answered Ken evasively.

"I thought so. Did you ever hear of the bowl fight, the great event of the year here at Wayne University?"

"Yes, I've heard—read a little about it. But I don't know what it is."

"I'll tell you," went on Dale. "There are a number of yearly rushes and scrapes between the freshmen and sophomores, but the bowl fight is the one big meeting, the time-honored event. It has been celebrated here for many years. It takes place on a fixed date. Briefly, here's what comes off: The freshmen have the bowl in their keeping this year because they won it in the last fight. They are to select one of their number, always a scrappy fellow, and one honored by the class, and they call him the bowl man. A week before the fight, on a certain date, the freshmen hide this bowl man or protect him from the sophomores until the day of the fight, when they all march to Grant Field in fighting togs. Should the sophomores chance to find him and hold him prisoner until after the date of the bowl fight, they win the bowl. The same applies also in case the bowl is in possession of the sophomores. But for ten years neither class has captured the other's bowl man. So they have fought it out on the field until the bowl was won."

"Well, what has all that got to do with me?" asked Ken. He felt curiously light-headed.

"It has a *little* to do with you—hasn't it, fellows?" said Dale, in slow, tantalizing voice.

Worry Arthurs lost his worried look and began to smile and rub his hands.

"Ward, look here," added Dale, now speaking sharply. "You've been picked for the bowl man!"

"Me—me?" stammered Ken.

"No other. The freshmen were late in choosing a man this year. Today, after your stunt—holding up that bunch of sophomores—they had a meeting in Carlton Hall and picked you. Most of them didn't even know your name. I'll bet the whole freshman class is hunting for you right now."

"What for?" queried Ken, weakly.

"Why, I told you. The bowl fight is only a week off—and here you are. *And here you'll stay until that date's past!*"

Ken drew a quick breath. He began to comprehend. The sudden huzzahs of Dale's companions gave him further enlightenment.

"But, Captain Dale," he said breathlessly, "if it's so—if my class has picked me—I can't throw them down. I don't know a soul in my class. I haven't a friend. But I won't throw them down— not to be forever free of dodging Sophs—not even to square myself with you."

"Ward, you're all right!" shouted Dale, his eyes shining.

In the quiet moment that followed, with all the sophomores watching him intently, Ken Ward instinctively felt that his measure had been taken.

"I won't stay here," said Ken, and for the first time his voice rang.

"Oh yes, you will," replied Dale, laughing.

Quick as a cat Ken leaped for the door and got it unlocked and half open before some one clutched him. Then Dale was on him close and hard. Ken began to struggle. He was all muscle, and twice he broke from them.

"His legs! Grab his legs! He's a young bull!"

"We'll trim you now, Freshie!"

"You potato-masher!"

"Go for his wind!"

Fighting and wrestling with all his might Ken went down under a half dozen sophomores. Then Dale was astride his chest, and others were sitting on his hands and feet.

"Boys, don't hurt that arm!" yelled Arthurs.

"Ward, will you be good now and stop scrapping or shall we tie you?" asked Dale. "You can't get away. The thing to do is to give your word not to try. We want to make this easy for you. Your word of honor, now?"

"Never!" cried Ken.

"I knew you wouldn't," said Dale. "We'll have to keep you under guard."

They let him get up. He was panting, and his nose was bleeding, and one of his knuckles was skinned. That short struggle had been no joke. The Sophs certainly meant to keep him prisoner. Still, he was made to feel at ease. They could not do enough for him.

"It's tough luck, Ward, that you should have fallen into our hands this way," said Dale. "But you couldn't help it. You will be kept in my rooms until after the fifteenth. Meals will be brought you, and your books; everything will be done for your comfort. Your whereabouts, of course, will be a secret, and you will be closely watched. Worry, remember you are bound to silence. And Ward, perhaps it wasn't an ill wind that blew you here. You've had your last scrap with a Soph, that's sure. As for what brought you here—it's more than square; and I'll say this: If you can play ball as well as you can scrap, old Wayne has got a star."

·4·

THE CALL FOR CANDIDATES

THERE were five rooms in Dale's suite in the dormitory, and three other sophomores shared them with him. They confined Ken in the end room, where he was safely locked and guarded from any possible chance to escape.

For the first day or two it was irksome for Ken; but as he and his captors grew better acquainted the strain eased up, and Ken began to enjoy himself as he had not since coming to the university.

He could not have been better provided for. His books were at hand, and even notes of the lectures he was missing were brought to him. The college papers and magazines interested him, and finally he was much amused by an account of his mysterious disappearance. All in a day he found himself famous. Then Dale and his roommates were so friendly and jolly that if his captivity had not meant the disgrace of the freshman class, Ken would have rejoiced in it. He began to thaw out, though he did not lose his backwardness. The life of the great university began to be real to him.

Almost the whole sophomore class, in squads of twos and threes and sixes, visited Dale's rooms during that week. No Soph wanted to miss a sight of a captive bowl man. Ken felt so callow and fresh in their presence that he scarcely responded to their jokes. Worry Arthur's nickname of "Kid" vied with another the coach conferred on Ken, and that was "Peg." It was significant slang expressing the little baseball man's baseball notion of Ken's throwing power.

The evening was the most interesting time for Ken. There was always something lively going on. He wondered when the boys studied. When some of the outside students dropped in, there was banjo and guitar playing, college songs, and college gossip.

"Come on, Peg, be a good fellow," they said, and laughed at his refusal to smoke or drink beer.

"Sissy!" mocked one.

"Mama's boy!" added another.

Ken was callow, young, and backward; but he had a temper, and this kind of banter roused it easily. The red flamed into his cheeks.

"I promised my mother I wouldn't smoke or drink or gamble while I was in college," he retorted, struggling with shame and anger. "And I—I won't."

Dale stopped the good-natured chaff. "Fellows, stop making fun of Ward; cut it out, I tell you. He's only a kid freshman, but he's liable to hand you a punch, and if he does you'll remember it. Besides, he's right. . . . Look here, Ward, you stick to that promise. It's a good promise to stick to, and if you're going in for athletics it's the best ever."

Worry Arthurs happened to be present on this evening, and he seconded Dale in more forceful speech. "There's too much boozin' and smokin' of them coffin nails goin' on in this college. It's none of my affair except with the boys I'm coachin', and if I ketch anyone breakin' my rules after we go to the trainin' table he'll sit on the bench. There's Murray; why, he says there are fellows in college who could break records if they'd train. Half of sprintin' or baseball or football is condition."

"Oh, Worry, you and Mac always make a long face over things. Wayne has won a few championships, hasn't she?"

"The varsity ball team will be a bust this year, that's sure," replied Arthurs, gloomily.

"How do you make that out?" demanded Dale, plainly nettled. "You've hinted at it before to me. Why won't we be stronger than last season? Didn't we have a crackerjack team, the fastest that ever represented old Wayne? Didn't we smother the small college teams and beat Place twice, shut out Herne the first game, and play for a tie the second?"

"You'll see, all right, all right," replied Arthurs,

gloomier than ever; and he took his hat and went out.

Dale slammed his cards down on the table.

"Fellows, is it any wonder we call him Worry? Already he's begun to fuss over the team. Ever since he's been here he has driven the baseball captains and managers crazy. It's only his way, but it's so irritating. He's a magnificent coach, and Wayne owes her great baseball teams to him. But he's hard on captains. I see my troubles. The idea of this year's team being a bust—with all the old stars back in college—with only two positions to fill! And there are half a dozen cracks in college to fight for these two positions—fellows I played against on the independent summer teams last year. Worry's idea is ridiculous."

This bit of baseball talk showed Ken the obstacles in the way of a freshman making the varsity team. What a small chance there would be for him! Still he got a good deal of comfort out of Arthurs' interest in him, and felt that he would be happy to play substitute this season, and make the varsity in his sophomore year.

The day of the bowl fight passed, and Ken's captivity became history. The biggest honor of the sophomore year went to Dale and his roommates. Ken returned to his department, where he was made much of, as he had brought fame to a new and small branch of the great university. It was a pleasure to walk the campus without fear of being pounced upon. Ken's dodging and lone-liness—perhaps necessary and curbing night-mares in the life of a freshman—were things of the past. He made acquaintances, slowly lost his backwardness, and presently found college life opening to him bright and beautiful. Ken felt strongly about things. And as his self-enforced exile had been lonely and bitter, so now his feeling that he was really a part of the great university seemed almost too good to be true. He began to get a glimmering of the meaning of his father's love for the old college. Students and professors underwent some vague change in his mind. He could not tell what, he did not think much about it, but there was a warmer touch, a sense of some-thing nearer to him.

Then suddenly a blow fell upon the whole un-dergraduate body. It was a thunderbolt. It af-fected every student, but Ken imagined it concerned his own college fortunes more inti-mately. The athletic faculty barred every member of the varsity baseball team! The year before the faculty had advised and requested the players not to become members of the independent, semi-professional summer baseball teams. Their wishes had not been heeded. Captain Dale and his fast players had been much in demand by the famous summer nines. Some of them went to the Orange Athletic Club, others to Richfield Springs, others to Cape May, and Dale himself had captained the Atlantic City team.

The action of the faculty was commended by the college magazine. Even the students, though chafing under it, could not but acknowledge its justice. The other universities had adopted such a rule, and Wayne had to fall in line. The objections to summer ball-playing were not few, and the particular one was that it affected the amateur standing of the college player. He became open to charges of professionalism. At least, all his expenses were paid, and it was charged that usually he was paid for his services.

Ken's first feeling when he learned this news was one of blank dismay. The great varsity team wiped off the slate! How Place and Herne would humble old Wayne this year! Then the long, hard schedule, embracing thirty games, at least one with every good team in the East—how would an untried green team fare against that formidable array? Then Ken suddenly felt ashamed of a selfish glee, for he was now sure of a place on the varsity.

For several days nothing else was talked about by the students. Whenever Dale or his players appeared at Carlton Hall they were at once surrounded by a sympathetic crowd. If it was a bitter blow to the undergraduates, what was it to the members of the varsity? Their feeling showed in pale, stern faces. It was reported about the campus that Murray and Arthurs and Dale, with the whole team, went to the directors of the athletic faculty and begged them to change or modify the decision. Both the trainer and the coach, who had brought such glory to the university, threatened to resign their places. The disgrace of a pitiably weak team of freshmen being annihilated by minor colleges was eloquently put before the directors. But the decision was final.

One evening early in February Worry Arthurs called upon Ken. His face was long, and his mustache drooped.

"Kid, what do you think of them fatheads on the faculty throwin' out my team?" he asked. "Best team I ever developed. Say, but the way they could work the hit-and-run game! Any man on the team could hit to right field when there was a runner goin' down from first."

"Maybe things will turn out all right," suggested Ken hopefully.

Worry regarded his youthful sympathizer with scorn.

"It takes two years to teach most college kids the rudiments of baseball. Look at this year's schedule." Worry produced a card and waved it at Ken. "The hardest schedule Wayne ever had! And I've got to play a kid team."

Ken was afraid to utter any more of his hopes, and indeed he felt them to be visionary.

"The call for candidates goes out tomorrow,"

went on the coach. "I'll bet there'll be a mob at the cage. Every fool kid in the university will think he's sure of a place. Now, Ward, what have you played?"

"Everywhere; but infield mostly."

"Every kid has played the whole game. What position have you played most?"

"Third base."

"Good! You've the arm for that. Well, I'm anxious to see you work, but don't exert yourself in the cage. This is a tip. See! I'll be busy weedin' out the bunch and won't have time until we get out on the field. You can run around the track every day, get your wind and your legs right, hold in on your arm. The cage is cold. I've seen many a good wing go bad there. But your chances look good. College baseball is different from any other kind. You might say it's played with the heart. I've seen youngsters go in through grit and spirit, love of playin' for their college, and beat out fellows who were their superiors physically. Well, good night. . . . Say, there's one more thing. I forgot it. Are you up in your subjects?"

"I sure am," replied Ken. "I've had four months of nothing but study."

"The reason I ask is this: That faculty has made another rule, the one-year residence rule, they call it. You have to pass your exams, get your first year over, before you can represent any athletic club. So, in case I can use you on the team, you would have to go up for your exams two months or more ahead of time. That scare you?"

"Not a bit. I could pass mine right now," answered Ken confidently.

"Kid, you and me are goin' to get along. . . . Well, good night, and don't forget what I said."

Ken was too full of thoughts to speak; he could scarcely mumble good night to the coach. He ran upstairs three steps to the jump, and when he reached his room he did a war dance and ended by standing on his head. When he had gotten rid of his exuberance he sat down at once to write to his brother Hal about it, and also his forest ranger friend, Dick Leslie, with whom he had spent an adventurous time the last summer.

At Carlton Hall, next day, Ken saw a crowd of students before the bulletin board and, edging in, he read the following notice:

BASEBALL!

CALL FOR CANDIDATES FOR THE VARSITY BASEBALL TEAM

The Athletic Directors of the University earnestly request every student who can play ball, or who thinks he can, to present himself to Coach Arthurs at the cage on Feb. 3rd.

There will be no freshman team this year, and a new team entirely will be chosen for the varsity. Every student will have a chance. Applicants are requested to familiarize themselves with the new eligibility rules.

·5·

THE CAGE

KEN WARD dug down into his trunk for his old baseball suit and donned it with strange elation. It was dirty and torn, and the shoes that went with it were worn-out, but Ken was thinking of what hard ball-playing they represented. He put his overcoat on over his sweater, took up his glove, and sallied forth.

A thin coating of ice and snow covered the streets. Winter still whistled in the air. To Ken in his eagerness spring seemed a long way off. On his way across the campus he saw strings of uniformed boys making for Grant Field, and many wearing sweaters over their everyday clothes. The cage was situated at one end of the field apart from the other training quarters. When Ken got there he found a mob of players crowding to enter the door of the big barnlike structure. Others were hurrying away. Near the door a man was taking up tickets like a doorkeeper of a circus, and he kept shouting: "Get your certificates from the doctor. Every player must pass a physical examination. Get your certificates."

Ken turned somewhat in disgust at so much red tape, and he jostled into a little fellow, almost knocking him over.

"Wull! Why don't you fall all over me?" growled this amiable individual. "For two cents I'd hand you one."

The apology on Ken's lips seemed to halt of its own accord.

"Sorry, I haven't any change in these clothes," returned Ken. He saw a wiry chap, older than he was, but much smaller, and of most aggressive front. He had round staring eyes, a protruding jaw, and his mouth turned down at the corners. He wore a disreputable uniform and a small green cap over one ear.

"Aw! don't get funny!" he replied.

Ken moved away, muttering to himself: "That fellow's a grouch." Much to his amazement, when he got to the training house, Ken found that he could not get inside because so many players were there ahead of him. After waiting an hour or more he decided he could not have his physical examination at that time, and he went back to the cage. The wide door was still blocked with players, but at the other end of the building Ken found an entrance. He squeezed into a crowd of students and worked forward until stopped by a railing.

Ken was all eyes and breathless with interest.

The cage was a huge, open, airy room, lighted by many windows, and, with the exception of the platform where he stood, it was entirely enclosed by heavy netting. The floor was of bare ground, well raked and loosened to make it soft. This immense hall was full of a motley crowd of aspiring ballplayers.

Worry Arthurs, with his head sunk in the collar of his overcoat, and his shoulders hunched up as if he was about to spring upon something, paced up and down the rear end of the cage. Behind him a hundred or more players in line slowly marched toward the slab of rubber which marked the batting position. Ken remembered that the celebrated coach always tried out new players at the bat first. It was his belief that batting won games.

"Bunt one and hit one!" he yelled to the batters.

From the pitcher's box a lanky individual was trying to locate the plate. Ken did not need a second glance to see that this fellow was no pitcher.

"Stop posin', and pitch!" yelled Arthurs.

One by one the batters faced the plate, swung valiantly or wildly at balls and essayed bunts. Few hit the ball out and none made a creditable bunt. After their turn at bat they were ordered to the other end of the cage, where they fell over one another trying to stop the balls that were hit. Every few moments the coach would yell for one of them, anyone, to take a turn at pitching. Ken noticed that Arthurs gave a sharp glance at each new batter, and one appeared to be sufficient. More and more ambitious players crowded into the cage, until there were so many that batted balls rarely missed hitting someone.

Presently Ken Ward awoke from his thrilling absorption in the scene to note another side of it. The students around him were making game of the players.

"What a bunch!"

"Look at that fuzzy gosling with the yellow pants!"

"Keep your shanks out of the way, Freshie!"

"Couldn't hit a balloon!"

Whenever a batter hit a ball into the crowd of dodging players down the cage these students howled with glee. Ken discovered that he was standing near Captain Dale and other members of the barred varsity.

"Say, Dale, how do the candidates shape up?" asked a student.

"This is a disgrace to Wayne," declared Dale, bitterly. "I never saw such a mob of spindle-legged kids in my life. Look at them! Scared to death! That fellow never swung at a ball before—that one never heard of a bunt—they throw like girls—oh! this is sickening, fellows. I see where Worry goes to his grave this year and old Wayne gets humbled by one-horse colleges."

Ken took one surprised glance at the captain he had admired so much and then he slipped farther over in the crowd. Perhaps Dale had spoken truth, yet somehow it jarred upon Ken's sensitive nature. The thing that affected Ken most was the earnestness of the uniformed boys trying their best to do well before the great coach. Some were timid, uncertain; others were rash and over-zealous. Many a ball cracked off a player's knee or wrist, and more than once Ken saw a bloody finger. It was cold in the cage. Even an ordinarily hit ball must have stung the hands, and the way a hard grounder cracked was enough to excite sympathy among those scornful spectators, if nothing more. But they yelled in delight at every fumble, at everything that happened. Ken kept whispering to himself: "I can't see the fun in it. I can't!"

Arthurs dispensed with the bunting and ordered one hit each for the batters. "Step up and hit!" he ordered hoarsely. "Don't be afraid— never mind that crowd—step into the ball and swing natural. . . . Next! Hurry, boys!"

Suddenly a deep-chested student yelled out with a voice that drowned every other sound.

"Hard luck, Worry! No use! You'll never find a hitter among those misfits!"

The coach actually leaped up in his anger and his face went from crimson to white. Ken thought it was likely that he recognized the voice.

"You knocker! You knocker!" he cried. "That's a fine college spirit, ain't it? A fine lot of students you are! Now shut up, every one of you, or I'll throw you out of the cage. . . . And right here at the start you knockers take this from me—I'll find more than one hitter among those kids!"

A little silence fell while the coach faced that antagonistic crowd of spectators. Ken was amazed the second time, and now because of the intensity of feeling that seemed to hang in the air. Ken felt a warm rush go over him, and that moment added greatly to his already strong liking for Worry Arthurs.

Then the coach turned to his work, the batting began again, and the crack of the ball, the rush of feet, the sharp cries of the players mingled once more with the laughter and caustic wit of the unsympathetic audience.

Ken Ward went back to his room without having removed his overcoat. He was thoughtful that night and rebellious against the attitude of the student body. A morning paper announced the fact that over three hundred candidates had presented themselves to Coach Arthurs. It went on to say that the baseball material represented was not worth considering and that old Wayne's varsity team must be ranked with those of the fifth-rate colleges. This, following Ken's experience at the cage on the first day, made him angry and then depressed. The glamour of the thing seemed to fade away. Ken lost the glow, the exhilaration of his first feelings. Everybody took a hopeless view of Wayne's baseball prospects. Ken Ward, however, was not one to stay discouraged long, and when he came out of his gloom it was with his fighting spirit roused. Once and for all he made up his mind to work heart and soul for his college, to be loyal to Arthurs, to hope and believe in the future of the new varsity, whether or not he was lucky enough to win a place upon it.

Next day, going early to the training quarters, he took his place in a squad waiting for the physical examination. It was a wearisome experience. At length Ken's turn came with two other players, one of whom he recognized as the sour-complexioned fellow of the day before.

"Wull, you're pretty fresh," he said to Ken as they went in. He had a most exasperating manner.

"Say, I don't like you a whole lot," retorted Ken.

Then an attendant ushered them into a large room in which were several men. The boys were stripped to the waist.

"Come here, Murray," said the doctor. "There's some use in looking these boys over, particularly this husky youngster."

A tall man in a white sweater towered over Ken. It was the famous trainer. He ran his hands over Ken's smooth skin and felt of the muscles.

"Can you run?" he asked.

47

"Yes," replied Ken.

"Are you fast?"

"Yes."

Further inquiries brought from Ken his name, age, weight, that he had never been ill, had never used tobacco or intoxicating drinks.

"Ward, eh? 'Peg' Ward," said Murray, smiling. "Worry Arthurs has the call on you—else, my boy, I'd whisper football in your ear. Mebbe I will, anyhow, if you keep up in your studies. That'll do for you."

Ken's companions also won praise from the trainer. They gave their names as Raymond and Weir. The former weighed only one hundred and twenty-two, but he was a knot of muscles. The other stood only five feet, but he was very broad and heavy, his remarkably compact build giving an impression of great strength. Both replied in the negative to the inquiries as to use of tobacco or spirits.

"Boys, that's what we like to hear," said the doctor. "You three ought to pull together."

Ken wondered what the doctor would have said if he had seen the way these three boys glared at each other in the dressing room. And he wondered, too, what was the reason for such open hostility. The answer came to him in the thought that perhaps they were both trying for the position he wanted on the varsity. Most likely they had the same idea about him. That was the secret of little Raymond's pugnacious front and Weir's pompous air; and Ken realized that the same reason accounted for his own attitude toward them. He wanted very much to tell Raymond that he was a little grouch and Weir that he looked like a puffed-up toad. All the same Ken was not blind to Weir's handsome appearance. The sturdy youngster had an immense head, a great shock of bright brown hair, flashing gray eyes, and a clear bronze skin.

"They'll both make the team, I'll bet," thought Ken. "They look it. I hope I don't have to buck against them." Then as they walked toward the cage Ken forced himself to ask genially: "Raymond, what're you trying for? And you, Weir?"

"Wull, if it's any of your fresh business, I'm not *trying* for any place. I'm going to play infield. You can carry my bat," replied Raymond sarcastically.

"Much obliged," retorted Ken, "I'm not going to substitute. I've a corner on that varsity infield myself."

Weir glanced at them with undisguised disdain. "You can save yourselves useless work by not trying for my position. I intend to play infield."

"Wull now, aren't we puffed up," growled Raymond.

Thus the three self-appointed stars of the varsity bandied words among themselves as they crossed the field. At the cage door they became separated to mingle with the pushing crowd of excited boys in uniforms.

By dint of much squeezing and shoulder work Ken got inside the cage. He joined the squad in the upper end and got in line for the batting. Worry Arthurs paced wildly to and fro, yelling for the boys to hit. A dense crowd of students thronged the platform and laughed, jeered, and stormed at the players. The cage was in such an uproar that Arthurs could scarcely be heard. Watching from the line Ken saw Weir come to bat and stand aggressively and hit the ball hard. It scattered the flock of fielders. Then Raymond came along, and, batting left-handed, did likewise. Arthurs stepped forward and said something to both. After Ken's turn at bat the coach said to him: "Get out of here. Go run around the track. Do it every day. Don't come back until Monday."

As Ken hurried out he saw and felt the distinction with which he was regarded by the many players whom he crowded among in passing. When he reached the track he saw Weir, Raymond, and half a dozen other fellows going around at a jog trot. Weir was in the lead, setting the pace. Ken fell in behind.

The track was the famous quarter-mile track upon which Murray trained his sprinters. When Ken felt the spring of the cinder path in his feet, the sensation of buoyancy, the eager wildfire pride that flamed over him, he wanted to break into headlong flight. The first turn around the track was delight; the second, pleasure in his easy stride; the third brought a realization of distance. When Ken had trotted a mile he was not tired, he still ran easily, but he began to appreciate that his legs were not wings. The end of the second mile found him sweating freely and panting.

Two miles were enough for the first day. Ken knew it and he began to wonder why the others, especially Weir, did not know it. But Weir jogged on, his head up, his hair flying, as if he had not yet completed his first quarter. The other players stretched out behind him. Ken saw Raymond's funny little green cap bobbing up and down, and it made him angry. Why couldn't the grouch get a decent cap, anyway?

At the end of the third mile, Ken began to labor. His feet began to feel weighted, his legs to ache, his side to hurt. He was wringing wet; his skin burned; his breath whistled. But he kept doggedly on. It had become a contest now. Ken felt instinctively that every runner would not admit he had less staying power than the others. Ken declared to himself that he could be as bullheaded as any of them. Still to see Weir jogging on steady and strong put a kind of despair on Ken. For every lap of the fourth mile a runner dropped out, and at the half of the fifth only Weir, Raymond, and Ken kept to the track.

Ken hung on gasping at every stride. He was afraid his heart would burst. The pain in his side was as keen as a knife thrust. His feet were lead. Every rod he felt must be his last, yet he spurred on desperately, and he managed to keep at the heels of the others. It might kill him, but he would not stop until he dropped. Raymond was wagging along, ready to fall any moment, and Weir was trotting slowly with head down. On the last lap of the fifth mile they all stopped as by one accord. Raymond fell on the grass; Ken staggered to a bench, and Weir leaned hard against the fence. They were all blowing like porpoises and regarded each other as mortal enemies. Weir gazed grandly at the other two; Raymond glowered savagely at him and then at Ken; and Ken in turn gave them withering glances. Without a word the three contestants for a place on the varsity then went their several ways.

· 6 ·

OUT ON THE FIELD

WHEN Ken presented himself at the cage on the following Monday it was to find that Arthurs had weeded out all but fifty of the candidates. Every afternoon for a week the coach put these players through batting and sliding practice, then ordered them out to run around the track. On the next Monday only twenty-five players were left, and as the number narrowed down the work grew more strenuous, the rivalry keener, and the tempers of the boys more irascible.

Ken discovered it was work and not by any means pleasant work. He fortified himself by the thought that the pleasure and glory, the real play, was all to come as a reward. Worry Arthurs drove them relentlessly. Nothing suited him; not a player knew how to hold a bat, to stand at the plate, to slide right, or to block a ground ball.

"Don't hit with your left hand on top—unless you're left-handed. Don't grip the end of the bat. There! Hold steady now, step out and into the ball, and swing clean and level. If you're afraid of bein' hit by the ball, get out of here!"

It was plain to Ken that not the least of Arthurs's troubles was the incessant gibing of the students on the platform. There was always a crowd watching the practice, noisy, scornful, abusive. They would never recover from the shock of having that seasoned champion varsity barred out of athletics. Every once in a while one of them would yell out: "Wait, Worry! oh! Worry, wait till the old varsity plays your scrubs!" And every time the coach's face would burn. But he had ceased to talk back to the students. Besides, the athletic directors were always present. They mingled with the candidates and talked baseball to them and talked to Arthurs. Some of them might have played ball once, but they did not talk like it. Their advice and interference served only to make the coach's task harder.

Another Monday found only twenty players in the squad. That day Arthurs tried out catchers, pitchers, and infielders. He had them all throwing, running, fielding, working like Trojans. They would jump at his yell, dive after the ball, fall over it, throw it anywhere but in the right direction, run wild, and fight among themselves. The ever-flowing ridicule from the audience was anything but a stimulus. So much of it coming from the varsity and their adherents kept continually in the minds of the candidates their lack of skill, their unworthiness to represent the great university in such a popular sport as baseball. So that even if there were latent ability in any of the candidates no one but the coach could see it. And often he could not conceal his disgust and hopelessness.

"Battin' practice!" he ordered sharply. "Two hits and a bunt today. Get a start on the bunt and dig for first. Hustle now!"

He appointed one player to pitch to the hitters, another to catch, and as soon as the hitters had their turn they took to fielding. Two turns for each at bat left the coach more than dissatisfied.

"You're all afraid of the ball," he yelled. "This ain't no dodgin' game. Duck your head if the ball's goin' to hit you, but stop lookin' for it. Forget it. Another turn now. I'm goin' to umpire. Let's see if you know the difference between a ball and a strike."

He changed the catcher and, ordering Ken to the pitcher's box, he stepped over behind him. "Peg," he said, speaking low, "you're not tryin' for pitcher, I know, but you've got speed and control and I want you to peg 'em a few. Mind now, easy with your arm. By that I mean hold in, don't whip it. And you peg 'em as near where I say as you can, see?"

As the players, one after another, faced the box, the coach kept saying to Ken: "Drive that fellow away from the plate . . . give this one a low ball . . . now straight over the pan. Say, Peg, you've got a nice ball there . . . put a fast one under this fellow's chin."

"Another turn, now, boys!" he yelled. "I tell you—*stand up to the plate!*" Then he whispered to Ken. "Hit every one of 'em! Peg 'em now, any place."

"Hit them?" asked Ken, amazed.

"That's what I said."

"But—Mr. Arthurs—"

"See here, Peg. Don't talk back to me. Do as I say. We'll peg a little nerve into this bunch. Now I'll go back of the plate and make a bluff."

Arthurs went near to the catcher's position. Then he said: "Now, fellows, Ward's pretty wild and I've told him to speed up a few. Stand right up and step into 'em."

The first batter was Weir. Ken swung easily and let drive. Straight as a string the ball sped for the batter. Like a flash he dropped flat in the dust and the ball just grazed him. It was a narrow escape. Weir jumped up, his face flaring, his hair on end, and he gazed hard at Ken before picking up the bat.

"Batter up!" ordered the coach. "Do you think this is a tea party?"

Weir managed by quick contortions to get through his time at bat without being hit. Three players following him were not so lucky.

"Didn't I say he was wild?" yelled the coach. "Batter up, now!"

The next was little Raymond. He came forward cautiously, eyeing Ken with disapproval. Ken could not resist putting on a little more steam, and the wind of the first ball whipped off Raymond's green cap. Raymond looked scared and edged away from the plate, and as the second ball came up he stepped wide with his left foot.

"Step into the ball," said the coach. "Don't pull away. Step in or you'll never hit."

The third ball cracked low down on Raymond's leg.

"Oh!—oh!—oh!" he howled, beginning to hop and hobble about the cage.

"Next batter!" called out Arthurs.

And so it went on until the most promising player in the cage came to bat. This was Graves, a light-haired fellow, tall, built like a wedge. He had more confidence than any player in the squad and showed up well in all departments of the game. Moreover, he was talky, aggressive, and more inclined to be heard and felt. He stepped up and swung his bat at Ken.

"You wild freshman! If you hit me!" he cried.

Ken Ward had not fallen in love with any of his rivals for places on the team, but he especially did not like Graves. He did not stop to consider the reason for it at the moment; still, he remembered several tricks Graves had played, and he was not altogether sorry for the coach's order. Swinging a little harder, Ken threw straight at Graves.

"*Wham!*" The ball struck him fair on the hip. Limping away from the plate he shook his fist at Ken.

"Batter up!" yelled Arthurs. "A little more speed now, Peg. You see it ain't nothin' to get hit. Why, that's in the game. It don't hurt much. I never cared when I used to get hit. Batter up!"

Ken sent up a very fast ball, on the outside of the plate. The batter swung wide, and the ball, tipping the bat, glanced to one side and struck Arthurs in the stomach with a deep sound.

Arthurs' round face went red; he gurgled and gasped for breath; he was sinking to his knees when the yelling and crowing of the students on the platform straightened him up. He walked about a few minutes, then ordered sliding practice.

The sliding board was brought out. It was almost four feet wide and twenty long and covered with carpet.

"Run hard, boys, and don't let up just before you slide. Keep your speed and dive. Now at it!"

A line of players formed down the cage. The first one dashed forward and plunged at the board, hitting it with a bang. The carpet was slippery, and he slid off and rolled in the dust. The second player leaped forward and, sliding too soon, barely reached the board. One by one the others followed.

"Run fast now!" yelled the coach. "Don't flinch. . . . Go down hard and slide . . . light on your hands . . . keep your heads up . . . slide!"

This feature of cage work caused merriment among the onlookers. That sliding board was a wonderful and treacherous thing. Most players slid off it as swift as a rocket. Arthurs kept them running so fast and so close together that at times one would shoot off the board just as the next would strike it. They sprawled on the ground, rolled over, and rooted in the dust. One skinned his nose on the carpet; another slid the length of the board on his ear. All the time they kept running and sliding, the coach shouted to them, and the audience roared with laughter. But it was no fun for the sliders. Raymond made a beautiful slide, and Graves was good, but all the others were ludicrous.

It was a happy day for Ken, and for all the candidates, when the coach ordered them out on the field. This was early in March. The sun was bright, the frost all out of the ground, and a breath of spring was in the air. How different it was from the cold, gloomy cage! Then the mocking students, although more in evidence than before, were confined to the stands and bleachers, and could not so easily be heard. But the presence of the regular varsity team, practicing at the far end of Grant Field, had its effect on the untried players.

The coach divided his players into two squads and had them practice batting first, then fielding, and finally started them in a game, with each candidate playing the position he hoped to make on the varsity.

It was a weird game. The majority of the twenty candidates displayed little knowledge of baseball. Schoolboys on the commons could have beaten them. They were hooted and hissed by the students, and before half the innings were played the bleachers and stands were empty. That was what old Wayne's students thought of Arthurs's candidates.

In sharp contrast to most of them, Weir, Raymond, and Graves showed they had played the game somewhere. Weir at shortstop covered ground well, but he could not locate first base. Raymond darted here and there quick as a flash, and pounced upon the ball like a huge frog. Nothing got past him, but he juggled the ball. Graves was a finished and beautiful fielder; he was easy, sure, yet fast, and his throw from third to first went true as a line.

Graves's fine work accounted for Ken Ward's poor showing. Both were trying for third base, and when Ken once saw his rival play out on the field he not only lost heart and became confused, but he instinctively acknowledged that Graves was far his superior. After all his hopes and the kind interest of the coach it was a most bitter blow. Ken had never played so poor a game. The ball blurred in his tear-wet eyes and looked double. He did not field a grounder. He muffed foul flies and missed thrown balls. It did not occur to him that almost all of the players around him were in the same boat. He could think of nothing but the dashing away of his hopes. What was the use of trying? But he kept trying, and the harder he tried the worse he played. At the bat he struck out, fouled out, never hit the ball square at all. Graves got two well-placed hits to right field. Then when Ken was in the field Graves would come down the coaching line and talk to him in a voice no one else could hear.

"Fat chance *you've* got to make this team! Third base is my job, Freshie. Why, you towhead, you couldn't play marbles. You butterfingers, can't you stop anything? You can't even play sub on this team. Remember, Ward, I said I'd get you for hitting me that day. You hit me with a potato once, too. I'll chase you off this team."

For once Ken's spirit was so crushed and humbled that he could not say a word to his rival. He even felt he deserved it all. When the practice ended, and he was walking off the field with hanging head, trying to bear up under the blow, he met Arthurs.

"Hello! Peg," said the coach, "I'm going your way."

Ken walked along feeling Arthurs's glance upon him, but he was ashamed to raise his head.

"Peg, you were up in the air today—way off— you lost your head."

He spoke kindly and put his hand on Ken's arm. Ken looked up to see that the coach's face was pale and tired, with the characteristic worried look more marked than usual.

"Yes, I was," replied Ken impulsively. "I can play better than I did today—but—Mr. Arthurs, I'm not in Graves's class as a third baseman. I know it."

Ken said it bravely, though there was a catch in his voice. The coach looked closely at him.

"So you're sayin' a good word for Graves, pluggin' his game."

"I'd love to make the team, but old Wayne must have the best players you can get."

"Peg, I said once you and me were goin' to get along. I said also that college baseball is played with the heart. You lost your heart. So did most of the kids. Well, it ain't no wonder. This is a tryin' time. I'm playin' them against each other, and no fellow knows where he's at. Now, I've seen all along that you weren't a natural infielder. I played you at third today to get that idea out of your head. Tomorrow I'll try you in the outfield. You ain't no quitter, Peg."

Ken hurried to his room under the stress of a complete revulsion of feeling, though his liking for the coach began to grow into something more. It was strange to Ken what power a few words from Arthurs had to renew his will and hope and daring. How different Arthurs was when not on the field. There he was stern and sharp. Ken could not study that night, and he slept poorly. His revival of hope did not dispel his nervous excitement.

He went out into Grant Field next day fighting himself. When in the practice Arthurs assigned him to a right-field position, he had scarcely taken his place when he became conscious of a queer inclination to swallow often, of a numbing tight band around his chest. He could not stand still; his hands trembled; there was a mist before his eyes. His mind was fixed upon himself and upon the other five outfielders trying to make the team. He saw the players in the infield pace their positions restlessly, run without aim when the ball was hit or thrown, collide with each other, let the ball go between their hands and legs, throw wildly, and sometimes stand as if transfixed when they ought to have been in action. But all this was not significant to Ken. He saw everything that happened, but he thought only that he must make a good showing; he must not miss any flies, or let a ball go beyond him. He absolutely must do the right thing. The air of Grant Field was charged with intensity of feeling, and Ken thought it was all his own. His baseball fortune was at stake, and he worked himself into such a frenzy that if a ball had been batted in his direction he might not have seen it at all. Fortunately none came his way.

The first time at bat he struck out ignominiously, poking weakly at the pitcher's roundhouse curves. The second time he popped up a little fly. On the next attempt the umpire called him out on strikes. At his last chance Ken was desperate. He knew the coach placed batting before any other department of the game. Almost sick with the torture of the conflicting feelings, Ken went up to the plate and swung blindly. To his amazement he cracked a hard fly to left-center, far between the fielders. Like a startled deer Ken broke into a run. He turned first base and saw that he might stretch the hit into a three-bagger. He knew he could run, and never had he so exerted himself. Second base sailed under him, and he turned in line for the third. Watching Graves, he saw him run for the base and stand ready to catch the throw-in.

Without slackening his speed in the least Ken leaped into the air headlong for the base. He heard the crack of the ball as it hit Graves's glove. Then with a swift scrape on hands and breast he was sliding in the dust. He stopped suddenly as if blocked by a stone wall. Something hard struck him on the head. A blinding light within his brain seemed to explode into glittering slivers. A piercing pain shot through him. Then from darkness and a great distance sounded a voice:

"Ward, I said I'd get you!"

· 7 ·

ANNIHILATION

THAT incident put Ken out of the practice for
three days. He had a bruise over his ear as large
as a small apple. Ken did not mind the pain nor
the players' remarks that he had a swelled head
anyway, but he remembered with slowly gathering wrath Graves's words: "I said I'd get you!"

He remembered also Graves's reply to a question put by the coach. "I was only tagging him. I
didn't mean to hurt him." That rankled inside
Ken. He kept his counsel, however, even evading
a sharp query put by Arthurs, and as much as it
was possible he avoided the third baseman.

Hard practice was the order of every day, and
most of it was batting. The coach kept at the candidates everlastingly, and always his cry was: "Toe
the plate, left foot a little forward, step into the
ball and swing!" At the bat Ken made favorable
progress because the coach was always there behind him with encouraging words; in the field,
however, he made a mess of it and grew steadily
worse.

The directors of the Athletic Association had called upon the old varsity to go out and coach the new aspirants for college fame. The varsity had refused. Even the players of preceding years, what few were in or near the city, had declined to help develop Wayne's stripling team. But some of the older graduates, among them several of the athletic directors, appeared on the field. When Arthurs saw them he threw up his hands in rage and despair. That afternoon Ken had three well-meaning but old-fashioned ballplayers coach him in the outfield. He had them one at a time, which was all that saved him from utter distraction. One told him to judge a fly by the sound when the ball was hit. Another told him to play in close, and when the ball was batted to turn and run with it. The third said he must play deep and sprint in for the fly. Then each had different ideas as to how batters should be judged, about throwing to bases, about backing up the other fielders. Ken's bewilderment grew greater and greater. He had never heard of things they advocated, and he began to think he did not know anything about the game. And what made his condition of mind border on imbecility was a hurried whisper from Arthurs between innings: "Peg, don't pay the slightest attention to them fathead grad coaches."

Practice days succeeding that were worse nightmares to Ken Ward than the days he had spent in constant fear of the sophomores. It was a terribly feverish time of batting balls, chasing balls, and of having dinned into his ears thousands of orders, rules of play, talks on college spirit in athletics—all of which conflicted so that it was meaningless to him. During this dark time one ray of light was the fact that Arthurs never spoke a sharp word to him. Ken felt vaguely that he was whirling in some kind of a college athletic chaos, out of which he would presently emerge.

Toward the close of March the weather grew warm, the practice field dried up, and baseball should have been a joy to Ken. But it was not. At times he had a shameful wish to quit the field for good, but he had not the courage to tell the coach. The twenty-fifth, the day scheduled for the game with the disgraced varsity team, loomed closer and closer. Its approach was a fearful thing for Ken. Every day he cast furtive glances down the field to where the varsity held practice. Ken had nothing to say; he was as glum as most of the other candidates, but he had heard gossip in the lecture rooms, in the halls, on the street, everywhere, and it concerned this game. What would the old varsity do to Arthurs' new team? Curiosity ran as high as the feeling toward the athletic directors. Resentment flowed from every source. Ken somehow got the impression that he was blamable for being a member of the coach's green squad. So Ken Ward fluctuated between two fears, one as bad as the other—that he would not be selected to play, and the other that he would be selected. It made no difference. He would be miserable if not chosen, and if he was—how on earth would he be able to keep his knees from wobbling? Then the awful day dawned.

Coach Arthurs met all his candidates at the cage. He came late, he explained, because he wanted to keep them off the field until time for practice. Today he appeared more grave than worried, and where the boys expected a severe lecture, he simply said: "I'll play as many of you as I can. Do your best, that's all. Don't mind what these old players say. They were kids once, though they seem to have forgotten it. Try to learn from them."

It was the first time the candidates had been taken upon the regular diamond of Grant Field. Ken had peeped in there once to be impressed by the beautiful level playground, and especially the magnificent turreted grandstand and the great sweeping stretches of bleachers. Then they had been empty; now, with four thousand noisy students and thousands of other spectators besides, they stunned him. He had never imagined a crowd coming to see the game.

Perhaps Arthurs had not expected it either, for Ken heard him mutter grimly to himself. He ordered practice at once and called off the names of those he had chosen to start the game. As one in a trance Ken Ward found himself trotting out to right field.

A long-rolling murmur that was half laugh, half taunt, rose from the stands. Then it quickly subsided. From his position Ken looked for the players on the old varsity, but they had not yet come upon the field. Of the few balls batted to Ken in practice he muffed only one, and he was just beginning to feel that he might acquit himself creditably when the coach called the team in. Arthurs had hardly given his new players time enough to warm up, but likewise they had not had time to make any fumbles.

All at once a hoarse roar rose from the stands, then a thundering clatter of thousands of feet as the students greeted the appearance of the old varsity. It was applause that had in it all the feeling of the undergraduates for the championship team, many of whom they considered had been unjustly barred by the directors. Love, loyalty, sympathy, resentment—all pealed up to the skies in that acclaim. It rolled out over the heads of Arthurs' shrinking boys as they huddled together on the bench.

Ken Ward, for one, was flushing and thrilling. In that moment he lost his gloom. He watched the varsity come trotting across the field, a doughty band of baseball warriors. Each wore a sweater with the huge white "W" shining like a star. Many of those players had worn that honored varsity letter for three years. It did seem a shame to bar them from this season's team. Ken found himself thinking of the matter from their point of view, and his sympathy was theirs.

More than that, he gloried in the look of them, in the trained, springy strides, in the lithe, erect forms, in the assurance in every move. Every detail of that practice photographed itself upon Ken Ward's memory, and he knew he would never forget.

There was Dale, veteran player, captain and pitcher of the nine, hero of victories over Place and Herne. There was Hogan, catcher for three seasons, a muscular fellow, famed for his snap throw to the bases and his fiendish chasing of foul flies. There was Hickle, the great first baseman, whom the professional leagues were trying to get. What a reach he had; how easily he scooped in the ball; low, high, wide, it made no difference to him. There was Canton at second, Hollis at short, Burns at third, who had been picked for the last year's All-American College Team. Then there was Dreer, brightest star of all, the fleet, hard-hitting center fielder. This player particularly fascinated Ken. It was a beautiful sight to see him run. The ground seemed to fly behind him. When the ball was hit high he wheeled with his back to the diamond and raced out, suddenly to turn with unerring judgment—and the ball dropped into his hands. On low line drives he showed his fleetness, for he was like a gleam of light in his forward dash; and, however the ball presented itself, shoulder high, low by his knees, or on a short bound, he caught it. Ken Ward saw with despairing admiration what it meant to be a great outfielder.

Then Arthurs called "Play ball!" giving the old varsity the field.

With a violent start Ken Ward came out of his rhapsody. He saw a white ball tossed on the diamond. Dale received it from one of the fielders and took his position in the pitcher's box. The uniform set off his powerful form; there was something surly and grimly determined in his face. He glanced about to his players, as if from long habit, and called out gruffly: "Get in the game, fellows! No runs for this scrub outfit!" Then, with long-practiced swing, he delivered the ball. It traveled plateward as swift as the flight of a white swallow. The umpire called it a strike on Weir; the same on the next pitch; the third was wide. Weir missed the fourth and was out. Raymond followed on the batting list. Today, as he slowly stepped toward the plate, seemingly smaller and glummer than ever, it was plain he was afraid. The bleachers howled at the little green cap sticking over his ear. Raymond did not swing at the ball; he sort of reached out his bat at the first three pitches, stepping back from the plate each time. The yell that greeted his weak attempt seemed to shrivel him up. Also it had its effect on the youngsters huddling around Arthurs. Graves went up and hit a feeble grounder to Dale and was thrown out at first.

Ken knew the half-inning was over; he saw the varsity players throw aside their gloves and trot in. But either he could not rise or he was glued to the bench. Then Arthurs pulled him up, saying, "Watch sharp, Peg, these fellows are right-field hitters!" At the words all Ken's blood turned to ice. He ran out into the field fighting the coldest, most sickening sensation he had ever had in his life. The ice in his veins all went to the pit of his stomach and there formed into a heavy lump. Other times when he had been frightened flitted through his mind. It had been bad when he fought with Greaser, and worse when he ran with the outlaws in pursuit, and the forest fire was appalling. But Ken felt he would gladly have changed places at that moment. He dreaded the mocking bleachers.

Of the candidates chosen to play against the varsity Ken knew McCord at first, Raymond at second, Weir at short, Graves at third. He did not know even the names of the others. All of them, except Graves, appeared too young to play in that game.

Dreer was first up for the varsity, and Ken shivered all over when the lithe center fielder stepped to the left side of the plate. Ken went out deeper, for he knew most hard-hitting left-handers hit to right field. But Dreer bunted the first ball teasingly down the third-base line. Fleet as a deer, he was across the bag before the in-fielder reached the ball. Hollis was next up. On the first pitch, as Dreer got a fast start for second, Hollis bunted down the first-base line. Pitcher and baseman ran for the bunt; Hollis was safe, and the sprinting Dreer went to third without even drawing a throw. A long pealing yell rolled over the bleachers. Dale sent his coaches to the coaching lines. Hickle, big and formidable, hur-ried to the plate, swinging a long bat. He swung it as if he intended to knock the ball out of the field. When the pitcher lifted his arm Dreer dashed for home plate and seemed to be outracing the pitch. But Hickle deftly dumped it down the line and broke for first while Dreer scored. This bunt was not fielded at all. How the bleachers roared! Then followed bunts in rapid succession, dashes for first, and slides into the bag. The pitcher interfered with the third baseman, and the first baseman ran up the line, and the pitcher failed to cover the bag, and the catcher fell all over the ball. Every varsity man bunted, but in just the place where it was not expected. They raced around the bases. They made long runs from first to third. They were like flashes of light, slippery as eels. The bewildered infielders knew

they were being played with. The taunting boos
and screams of delight from the bleachers were
as demoralizing as the elusively daring runners.
Closer and closer the infielders edged in until
they were right on top of the batters. Then Dale
and his men began to bunt little infield flies over
the heads of their opponents. The merry audience
cheered wildly. But Graves and Raymond ran
back and caught three of these little pop flies,
thus retiring the side. The old varsity had made
six runs on nothing but deliberate bunts and daring dashes around the bases.

Ken hurried in to the bench and heard someone call out, "Ward up!"

He had forgotten he would have to bat. Stepping to the plate was like facing a cannon. One
of the players yelled: "Here he is, Dale! Here's
the potato pegger! Knock his block off!"

The cry was taken up by other players. "Peg
him, Dale! Peg him, Dale!" And then the bleachers got it. Ken's dry tongue seemed pasted to the
roof of his mouth. This Dale in baseball clothes
with the lowering frown was not like the Dale
Ken had known. Suddenly he swung his arm.
Ken's quick eye caught the dark, shooting gleam
of the ball. Involuntarily he ducked. "Strike,"
called the umpire. Then Dale had not tried to hit
him. Ken stepped up again. The pitcher whirled
slowly this time, turning with long, easy motion,
and threw underhand. The ball sailed, floated,

soared. Long before it reached Ken it had fooled him completely. He chopped at it vainly. The next ball pitched came up swifter, but just before it crossed the plate it seemed to stop, as if pulled back by a string, and then dropped down. Ken fell to his knees trying to hit it.

The next batter's attempts were not as awkward as Ken's; still, they were as futile. As Ken sat wearily down upon the bench he happened to get next to coach Arthurs. He expected some sharp words from the coach, he thought he deserved anything, but they were not forthcoming. The coach put his hand on Ken's knee. When the third batter fouled to Hickle, and Ken got up to go out to the field, he summoned courage to look at Arthurs. Something in his face told Ken what an ordeal this was. He divined that it was vastly more than business with Worry Arthurs.

"Peg, watch out this time," whispered the coach. "They'll line 'em at you this inning—like bullets. Now try hard, won't you? *Just try!*"

Ken knew from Arthurs's look more than his words that *trying* was all that was left for the youngsters. The varsity had come out early in the spring, and they had practiced to get into condition to annihilate this new team practically chosen by the athletic directors. And they had set out to make the game a farce. But Arthurs meant that all the victory was not in winning the game. It was left for his boys to try in the face of certain defeat, to try with all their hearts, to try with unquenchable spirit. It was the spirit that counted, not the result. The old varsity had received a bitter blow; they were aggressive and relentless. The students and supporters of old Wayne, idolizing the great team, always bearing in mind the hot rivalry with Place and Herne, were unforgiving and intolerant of an undeveloped varsity. Perhaps neither could be much blamed. But it was for the new players to show what it meant to them. The greater the prospect of defeat, the greater the indifference or hostility shown them, the more splendid their opportunity. For it was theirs to try for old Wayne, to try, to fight, and never to give up.

Ken caught fire with the flame of that spirit.

"Boys, come on!" he cried, in his piercing tenor. *"They can't beat us trying!"*

As he ran out into the field, members of the varsity spoke to him. "You green-backed freshman! Shut up! You scrub!"

"I'm not a varsity has-been!" retorted Ken, hurrying out to his position.

The first man up, a lefthander, rapped a hard twisting liner to right field. Ken ran toward deep center with all his might. The ball kept twisting and curving. It struck squarely in Ken's hands and bounced out and rolled far. When he recovered it the runner was on third base. Before Ken got back to his position the second batter hit

hard through the infield toward right. The ball
came skipping like a fiendish rabbit. Ken gritted
his teeth and went down on his knees, to get the
bounding ball full in his chest. But he stopped
it, scrambled for it, and made the throw in. Dale
likewise hit in his direction, a slow low fly, difficult
to judge. Ken overran it, and the hit gave Dale
two bases. Ken realized that the varsity was now
executing Worry Arthurs's famous right-field hitting. The sudden knowledge seemed to give Ken
the blind staggers. The field was in a haze; the
players blurred in his sight. He heard the crack
of the ball and saw Raymond dash over and plunge
down. Then the ball seemed to streak out of the
grass toward him, and, as he bent over, it missed
his hands and cracked on his shin. Again he fumbled wildly for it and made the throw in. The pain
roused his rage. He bit his lips and called to himself: "I'll stop them if it kills me!"

Dreer lined the ball over his head for a home
run. Hollis made a bid for a three-bagger, but
Ken, by another hard sprint, knocked the ball
down. Hickle then batted up a tremendously high
fly. It went far beyond Ken and he ran and ran.
It looked like a small pinpoint of black up in the
sky. Then he tried to judge it, to get under it.
The white sky suddenly glazed over and the ball
wavered this way and that. Ken lost it in the sun,
found it again, and kept on running. Would it
never come down? He had not reached it; he had

run beyond it. In an agony he lunged out, and the ball fell into his hands and jumped out.

Then followed a fusillade of hits, all between second base and first, and all vicious-bounding grounders. To and fro Ken ran, managing somehow to get some portion of his anatomy in front of the ball. It had become a demon to him now and he hated it. His tongue was hanging out, his breast was bursting, his hands were numb, yet he held before him the one idea to keep fiercely trying.

He lost count of the runs after eleven had been scored. He saw McCord and Raymond trying to stem the torrent of right-field hits, but those they knocked down gave him no time to recover. He blocked the grass-cutters with his knees or his body and pounced upon the ball and got it away from him as quickly as possible. Would this rapid fire of uncertain-bounding balls never stop? Ken was in a kind of frenzy. If he only had time to catch his breath!

Then Dreer was at bat again. He fouled the first two balls over the grandstand. Someone threw out a brand-new ball. Farther and farther Ken edged into deep right. He knew what was coming. "Let him—hit it!" he panted. "I'll try to get it! This day settles me. I'm no outfielder. But I'll try!"

The tired pitcher threw the ball and Dreer seemed to swing and bound at once with the ringing crack. The hit was one of his famous drives close to the right-field foul line.

Ken was off with all the speed left in him. He strained every nerve and was going fast when he passed the foul flag. The bleachers loomed up indistinct in his sight. But he thought only of meeting the ball. The hit was a savage liner, curving away from him. Cinders under his flying feet were a warning that he did not heed. He was on the track. He leaped into the air, left hand outstretched, and felt the ball strike in his glove.

Then all was dark in a stunning, blinding crash—

· 8 ·

EXAMINATIONS

WHEN Ken Ward came fully to his senses he was being half carried and half led across the diamond to the players' bench. He heard Worry Arthurs say: "He ain't hurt much—only butted into the fence."

Ken tried manfully to entertain Worry's idea about it, but he was too dazed and weak to stand alone. He imagined he had broken every bone in his body.

"Did I make the catch—hang on to the ball?" he asked.

"No, Peg, you didn't," replied the coach, kindly. "But you made a grand try for it."

He felt worse over failing to hold the ball than he felt over half killing himself against the bleachers. He spent the remainder of that never-to-be-forgotten game sitting on the bench. But to watch his fellow players try to play was almost as frightful as being back there in right field. It was no consolation for Ken to see his successor chasing long hits, misjudging flies, failing weakly on wicked grounders. Even Graves weakened toward the close and spoiled his good beginning by miserable fumbles and throws. It was a complete and disgraceful rout. The varsity never let up until the last man was out. The team could not have played harder against Place or Herne. Arthurs called the game at the end of the sixth inning with the score 41 to 0.

Many beaten and despondent players had dragged themselves off Grant Field in bygone years. But none had ever been so humiliated, so crushed. No player spoke a word or looked at another. They walked off with bowed heads. Ken lagged behind the others; he was still stunned and lame. Presently Arthurs came back to help him along, and did not speak until they were clear of the campus and going down Ken's street.

"I'm glad that's over," said Worry. "I kicked against havin' the game, but 'em fathead directors would have it. Now we'll be let alone. There won't be no students comin' out to the field, and I'm blamed glad."

Ken was sick and smarting with pain, and half crying.

"I'm sorry, Mr. Arthurs," he faltered, "we were—so—so—rotten!"

"See here, Peg," was the quick reply, "that cuts no ice with me. It was sure the rottenest exhibition I ever seen in my life. But there's excuses, and you can just gamble I'm the old boy who knows. You kids were scared to death. What hurts me, Peg, is the throw-down we got from my old team and from the students. We're not to blame for rules made by fathead directors. I was surprised at Dale. He was mean, and so were Hollis and Hickle—all of 'em. They didn't need to disgrace us like that."

"Oh, Mr. Arthurs, what players they are!" exclaimed Ken. "I never saw such running, such hitting. You said they'd hit to right field like bullets, but it was worse than bullets. And Dreer! . . . When he came up my heart just stopped beating."

"Peg, listen," said Worry. "Three years ago when Dreer came out on the field he was greener than you, and hadn't half the spunk. I made him what he is, and I made all of 'em—I made that team, and I can make another."

"You are just saying that to—to encourage me," replied Ken hopelessly. "I can't play ball. I thought I could, but I know now. I'll never go out on the field again."

"Peg, are you goin' to throw me down, too?"

"Mr. Arthurs! I—I—"

"Listen, Peg. Cut out the dumps. Get over 'em. You made the varsity today. Understand? You earned your big W. You needn't mention it, but I've picked you to play somewhere. You weren't a natural infielder, and you didn't make much of a showin' in the outfield. But it's the spirit I want.

Today was a bad day for a youngster. There's always lots of feelin' about college athletics, but here at Wayne this year the strain's awful. And you fought yourself and stage fright and the ridicule of 'em quitter students. You *tried*, Peg! I never saw a gamer try. You didn't fail me. And after you made that desperate run and tried to smash the bleachers with your face the students shut up their tauntin'. It made a difference, Peg. Even the varsity was a little ashamed. Cheer up, now!"

Ken was almost speechless; he managed to mumble something, at which the coach smiled in reply and then walked rapidly away. Ken limped to his room and took off his baseball suit. The skin had been peeled from his elbow, and his body showed several dark spots that Ken knew would soon be black-and-blue bruises. His legs from his knees down bore huge lumps so sore to the touch that Ken winced even at gentle rubbing. But he did not mind the pain. All the darkness seemed to have blown away from his mind.

"What a fine fellow Worry is!" said Ken. "How I'll work for him! I must write to brother Hal and Dick Leslie, to tell them I've made the varsity. . . . No, not yet; Worry said not to mention it. . . . And now to plug. I'll have to take my exams before the first college game, April 8, and that's not long."

In the succeeding days Ken was very busy with

attendance at college in the mornings, baseball practice in the afternoons, and study at night.

If Worry had picked any more players for the varsity, Ken could not tell who they were. Of course Graves would make the team, and Weir and Raymond were pretty sure of places. There were sixteen players for the other five positions, and picking them was only guesswork. It seemed to Ken that some of the players showed streaks of fast playing at times, and then as soon as they were opposed to one another in the practice game they became erratic. His own progress was slow. One thing he could do that brought warm praise from the coach—he could fire the ball home from deep outfield with wonderful speed and accuracy.

After the varsity had annihilated Worry's "kids," as they had come to be known, the students showed no further interest. When they ceased to appear on the field the new players were able to go at their practice without being ridiculed. Already an improvement had been noticeable. But rivalry was so keen for places, and the coach's choice so deep a mystery, that the contestants played under too great a tension, and high school boys could have done better.

It was on the first of April that Arthurs took Ken up into College Hall to get permission for him to present himself to the different professors for the early examinations. While Ken sat waiting in the office he heard Arthurs talking to men he instantly took to be the heads of the Athletic Association. They were in an adjoining room with the door open, and their voices were very distinct, so that Ken could not help hearing.

"Gentlemen, I want my answer today," said the coach.

"Is there so great a hurry? Wait a little," was the rejoinder.

"I'm sorry, but this is April 1, and I'll wait no longer. I'm ready to send some of my boys up for early exams, and I want to know where I stand."

"Arthurs, what is it exactly that you want? Things have been in an awful mess, we know. State your case and we'll try to give you a definite answer."

"I want full charge of the coachin'—the handlin' of the team, as I always had before. I don't want any grad coaches. The directors seem divided—one half want this, the other half that. They've cut out the trainin' quarters. I've had no help from Murray; no baths or rubdowns or trainin' for my candidates. Here's openin' day a week off and I haven't picked my team. I want to take them to the trainin' table and have them under my eye all the time. If I can't have what I want I'll resign. If I can I'll take the whole responsibility of the team on my own shoulders."

"Very well, Arthurs, we'll let you go ahead and have full charge. There has been talk this year of abolishing a private training house and table for this green varsity. But rather than have you resign we'll waive that. You can rest assured from now on you will not be interfered with. Give us the best team you can under the circumstances. There has been much dissension among the directors and faculty because of our new eligibility rules. It has stirred everybody up, and the students are sore. Then there has been talk of not having a professional coach this year, but we overruled that in last night's meeting. We're going to see what you can do. I may add, Arthurs, if you shape up a varsity this year that makes any kind of a showing against Place and Herne you will win the eternal gratitude of the directors who have fostered this change in athletics. Otherwise I'm afraid the balance of opinion will favor the idea of dispensing with professional coaches in the future."

Ken saw that Arthurs was white in the face when he left the room. They went out together, and Worry handed Ken a card that read for him to take his examinations at once.

"Are you up on 'em?" asked the coach anxiously.

"I—I think so," replied Ken.

"Well, Peg, good luck to you! Go at 'em like you went at Dreer's hit."

Much to his amazement it was for Ken to discover that, now that the time had come for him to face his examinations, he was not at all sanguine. He began to worry. He forgot about the textbooks he had mastered in his room during the long winter when he feared to venture out because of the sophomores. It was not very long till he had worked himself into a state somewhat akin to his trepidation in the varsity ballgame. Then he decided to go up at once and have it done with. His whole freshman year had been one long agony. What a relief to have it ended!

Ken passed four examinations in one morning, passed them swimmingly, smilingly, splendidly, and left College Hall in an ecstasy. Things were working out fine. But he had another examination, and it was in a subject he had voluntarily included in his course. Whatever on earth he had done it for he could not now tell. The old doctor who held the chair in that department had thirty years before earned the name of Crab. And slowly in the succeeding years he had grown crabbier, crustier, so student rumor had it. Ken had rather liked the dry old fellow, and had been much absorbed in his complex lectures, but he had never been near him, and now the prospect changed color. Foolishly Ken asked a sophomore in what light old Crab might regard a student who was ambitious to pass his exams early. The picture painted by that sophomore would have made a flaming-mouthed dragon appear tame. Nerving himself to the ordeal, Ken took his card and presented himself one evening at the doctor's house.

A maid ushered him into the presence of a venerable old man who did not look at all, even in Ken's distorted sight, like a crab or a dragon. His ponderous brow seemed as if it had all the thought in the world behind it. He looked over huge spectacles at Ken's card and then spoke in a dry, quavering voice.

"Um-m. Sit down, Mr. Ward."

Ken found his breath and strangely lost his fear and trembling. The doctor dryly asked him why he thought he knew more than the other students, who were satisfied to wait months longer before examination. Ken hastened to explain that it was no desire of his; that, although he had studied hard and had not missed many lectures, he knew he was unprepared. Then he went on to tell about the baseball situation and why he had been sent up.

"Um-m." The professor held a glass paperweight up before Ken and asked a question about it. Next he held out a ruler and asked something about that, and also a bottle of ink. Following this he put a few queries about specific gravity, atomic weight, and the like. Then he sat thrumming his desk and appeared far away in thought. After a while he turned to Ken with a smile that made his withered, parchment-like face vastly different.

"Where do you play?" he asked.

"S-sir?" stammered Ken.

"In baseball, I mean. What place do you play?

Catch? Thrower? I don't know the names much."

Ken replied eagerly, and then it seemed he was telling this stern old man all about baseball. He wanted to know what fouls were, and how to steal bases, and he was nonplussed by such terms as "hit-and-run." Ken discoursed eloquently on his favorite sport, and it was like a kind of dream to be there. Strange things were always happening to him.

"I've never seen a game," said the professor. "I used to play myself long ago, when we had a yarn ball and pitched underhand. I'll have to come out to the field some day. President Halstead, why, he likes baseball, he's a—a—what do you call it?"

"A fan—a rooter?" replied Ken, smiling.

"Um-m. I guess that's it. Well, Mr. Ward, I'm glad to meet you. You may go now."

Ken got up blushing like a girl. "But, Doctor, you were to—I was to be examined."

"I've examined you," he drawled, with a dry chuckle, and he looked over his huge spectacles at Ken. "I'll give you a passing mark. But, Mr. Ward, you know a heap more about baseball than you know about physics."

As Ken went out he trod upon air. What a splendid old fellow! The sophomore had lied. For that matter, when had a sophomore ever been known to tell the truth? But, he suddenly exclaimed, he himself was no longer a freshman.

He pondered happily on the rosy lining to his old cloud of gloom. How different things appeared after a little time. That old doctor's smile would linger long in Ken's memory. He felt deep remorse that he had ever misjudged him. He hurried on to Worry Arthurs's house to tell him the good news. And as he walked his mind was full with the wonder of it all—his lonely, wretched freshman days, now forever past; the slow change from hatred; the dawning of some strange feeling for the college and his teachers; and last, the freedom, the delight, the quickening stir in the present.

· 9 ·

PRESIDENT HALSTEAD ON COLLEGE SPIRIT

WAYNE'S opening game was not at all what Ken had dreamed it would be. The opposing team from Hudson School was as ill-assorted an aggregation as Ken had ever seen. They brought with them a small but noisy company of cheering supporters who, to the shame of Ken and his fellows, had the bleachers all to themselves. If any Wayne students were present they either cheered for Hudson or remained silent.

Hudson won, 9 to 2. It was a game that made Arthurs sag a little lower on the bench. Graves got Wayne's two tallies. Raymond at second played about all the game from the fielding standpoint. Ken distinguished himself by trying wildly and accomplishing nothing. When he went to his room that night he had switched back to his former spirits, and was disgusted with Wayne's ball team, himself most of all.

That was on a Wednesday. The next day rain prevented practice, and on Friday the boys were out on the field again. Arthurs shifted the players around, trying resignedly to discover certain positions that might fit certain players. It seemed to Ken that all the candidates, except one or two, were good at fielding and throwing, but when they came to play a game they immediately went into a trance.

Travers College was scheduled for Saturday. They had always turned out a good minor team, but had never been known to beat Wayne. They shut Arthurs' team out without a run. A handful of Wayne students sat in the bleachers mocking their own team. Arthurs used the two pitchers he had been trying hard to develop, and when they did locate the plate they were hit hard. Ken played or essayed to play right field for a while, but he ran around like a chicken with its head off, as a Travers player expressed it, and then Arthurs told him that he had better grace the bench the rest of the game. Ashamed as Ken was to be put out, he was yet more ashamed to feel that he was glad of it. Hardest of all to bear was the arrogant air put on by the Travers College players. Wayne had indeed been relegated to the fifth rank of college baseball teams.

On Monday announcements were made in all the lecture rooms and departments of the university, and bulletins were posted to the effect, that President Halstead wished to address the undergraduates in the Wayne auditorium on Tuesday at five o'clock.

Rumor flew about the campus and Carlton Hall, everywhere, that the president's subject would be "College Spirit," and it was believed he would have something to say about the present condition of athletics. Ken Ward hurried to the hall as soon as he got through his practice. He found the immense auditorium packed from pit to dome, and he squeezed into a seat on the steps.

The students, as always, were exchanging volleys of paper balls, matching wits, singing songs, and passing time merrily. When President Halstead entered, with two of his associates, he was greeted by a thunder of tongues, hands, and heels of the standing students. He was the best-beloved member of the university faculty, a distinguished, scholarly-looking man, well along in years.

He opened his address by declaring the need of college spirit in college life. He defined it as the vital thing, the heart of a great educational institution, and he went on to speak of its dangers, its fluctuations. Then he made direct reference to athletics in its relation to both college spirit and college life.

"Sport is too much with us. Of late years I have observed a great increase in the number of athletic students, and a great decrease in scholarship. The fame of the halfback and the shortstop and the oarsman has grown out of proportion to their real worth. The freshman is dazzled by it. The great majority of college men cannot shine in sport, which is the best thing that could be. The student's ideal, instead of achieving the highest scholarship, the best attainment for his career, is apt to be influenced by the honors and friendships that are heaped upon the great athlete. This is false to university life. You are here to prepare yourselves for the battle with the world, and I want to state that that battle is becoming more and more intellectual. The student who slights his studies for athletic glory may find himself, when that glory is long past, distanced in the race for success by a student who had not trained to run the hundred in ten seconds.

"But, gentlemen, to keep well up in your studies and *then* go in for athletics—that is entirely another question. It is not likely that any student who keeps to the front in any of the university courses will have too much time for football or baseball. I am, as you all know, heartily in favor of all branches of college sport. And that brings me to the point I want to make today. Baseball is my favorite game, and I have always been proud of Wayne's teams. The new eligibility rules, with which you are all familiar, were brought to me, and after thoroughly going over the situation I approved of them. Certainly it is obvious to you all that a university ballplayer making himself famous here, and then playing during the summer months at a resort, is laying himself open to suspicion. I have no doubt that many players are innocent of the taint of professionalism, but unfortunately they have become members of these summer teams after being first requested, then warned, not to do so.

"Wayne's varsity players of last year have been barred by the directors. They made their choice, and so should abide by it. They have had their day, and so should welcome the opportunity for younger players. But I am constrained to acknowledge that neither they nor the great body of undergraduates welcomed the change. This, more than anything, proves to me the evil of championship teams. The football men, the baseball men, the crew men, and all the student supporters want to win *all* the games *all* the time. I would like to ask you young gentlemen if you can take a beating? If you cannot, I would like to add that you are not yet fitted to go out into life. A good beating, occasionally, is a wholesome thing.

"Well, to come to the point now: I find, after studying the situation, that the old varsity players and undergraduates of this university have been lacking in—let us be generous and say, college spirit. I do not need to go into detail; suffice it to say that I know. I will admit, however, that I attended the game between the old varsity and the new candidates. I sat unobserved in a corner, and a more unhappy time I never spent in this university. I confess that my sympathies were with the inexperienced, undeveloped boys who were trying to learn to play ball. *Put yourselves in their places.* Say you are mostly freshmen, and you make yourselves candidates for the team because you love the game, and because you would love to bring honor to your college. You go out and try. You meet, the first day, an implacable team of skilled veterans who show their scorn of your poor ability, their hatred of your opportunity, and ride roughshod—I should say, run with spiked shoes—over you. You hear the roar of four thousand students applauding these hero veterans. You hear your classmates, your fellow students in Wayne, howl with ridicule at your weak attempts to compete with better, stronger players. . . . Gentlemen, how would you feel?

"I said before that college spirit fluctuates. If I did not know students well I would be deeply grieved at the spirit shown that day. I know that the tide will turn. . . . And, gentlemen, would not you and the old varsity be rather in an embarrassing position if—if these raw recruits should happen to develop into a team strong enough to cope with Place and Herne? Stranger things have happened. I am rather strong for the new players, not because of their playing, which is poor indeed, but for the way they *tried* under peculiarly adverse conditions.

"That young fellow Ward—what torture that inning of successive hard hits to his territory! I was near him in that end of the bleachers, and I watched him closely. Every attempt he made was a failure—that is, a failure from the point of view of properly fielding the ball. But, gentlemen, that day was not a failure for young Ward. It was a grand success. Someone said his playing was the poorest exhibition ever seen on Grant Field. That may be. I want to say that to my mind it was also the most splendid effort ever made on Grant Field. For it was made against defeat, fear, ridicule. It was an elimination of self. It was made for his coach, his fellow players, his college—that is to say, for the students who shamed themselves by scorn for his trial.

"Young men of Wayne, give us a little more of such college spirit!"

· 10 ·

NEW PLAYERS

WHEN practice time rolled around for Ken next day, he went upon the field once more with his hopes renewed and bright.

"I certainly do die hard," he laughed to himself. "But I can never go down and out now—never!"

Something seemed to ring in Ken's ears like peals of bells. In spite of his awkwardness Coach Arthurs had made him a varsity man; in spite of his unpreparedness old Crab had given him a passing mark; in spite of his unworthiness President Halstead had made him famous.

"I sure am the lucky one," said Ken for the hundredth time. "And now I'm going to force my luck." Ken had lately revolved in his mind a persistent idea that he meant to propound to the coach.

Ken arrived on the field a little later than usual, to find Arthurs for once minus his worried look. He was actually smiling, and Ken soon saw the reason for this remarkable change was the presence of a new player out in center field.

"Hello, Peg! Things are lookin' up," said the coach, beaming. "That's Homans out there in center—Roy Homans, a senior and a crackerjack ballplayer. I tried to get him to come out for the team last year, but he wouldn't spare the time. But he's goin' to play this season—said the president's little talk got him. He's a fast, heady, scientific player, just the one to steady you kids."

Before Ken could reply his attention was attracted from Homans to another new player in uniform now walking up to Arthurs. He was tall, graceful, powerful, had red hair, keen dark eyes, a clean-cut profile, and a square jaw.

"I've come out to try out for the team," he said, quietly, to the coach.

"You're a little late, ain't you?" asked Worry gruffly; but he ran a shrewd glance over the lithe form.

"Yes."

"Must have been stirred up by that talk of President Halstead's, wasn't you?"

"Yes." There was something quiet and easy about the stranger, and Ken liked him at once.

"Where do you play?" went on Worry.

"Left."

"Can you hit? Talk sense now, and mebbe you'll save me work. Can you hit?"

"Yes."

"Can you throw?"

"Yes." He spoke with quiet assurance.

100

"Can you run?" almost shouted Worry. He was nervous and irritable those days, and it annoyed him for unknown youths to speak calmly of such things.

"Run? Yes, a little. I did the hundred last year in nine and four-fifths."

"What! You can't kid me! Who are you?" cried Worry, getting red in the face. "I've seen you somewhere."

"My name's Ray."

"Say! Not *Ray*, the intercollegiate champion?"

"I'm the fellow. I talked it over with Murray. He kicked, but I didn't mind that. I promised to try to keep in shape to win the sprints at the intercollegiate meet."

"Say! Get out there in left field! Quick!" shouted Worry. . . . "Peg, hit him some flies. Lam 'em a mile! That fellow's a sprinter, Peg. What luck it would be if he can play ball! Hit 'em at him!"

Ken took the ball Worry tossed him, and, picking up a bat, began to knock flies out to Ray. The first few he made easy for the outfielder, and then he hit balls harder and off to the right or left. Without appearing to exert himself Ray got under them. Ken watched him and also kept the tail of his eye on Worry. The coach appeared to be getting excited, and he ordered Ken to hit the balls high and far away. Ken complied, but he could not hit a ball over Ray's head. He tried with all his strength. He had never seen a champion sprinter, and now he marveled at the wonderful stride.

"Oh! but his running is beautiful!" exclaimed Ken.

"That's enough! Come in here!" yelled Worry to Ray. "Peg, he makes Dreer look slow. I never saw as fast fieldin' as that."

When Ray came trotting in without seeming to be even warmed up, Worry blurted out: "You ain't winded—after all that? Must be in shape?"

"I'm always in shape," replied Ray.

"Pick up a bat!" shouted Worry. "Here, Duncan, pitch this fellow a few. Speed 'em, curve 'em, strike him out, hit him—anything!"

Ray was left-handed, and he stood up to the plate perfectly erect, with his bat resting quietly on his shoulder. He stepped straight, swung with an even, powerful swing, and he hit the first ball clear over the right-field bleachers. It greatly distanced Dreer's hit.

"What a drive!" gasped Ken.

"Oh!" choked Worry. "That's enough! You needn't lose my balls. Bunt one, now."

Ray took the same position, and as the ball came up he appeared to drop the bat upon it and dart away at the same instant.

Worry seemed to be trying to control violent emotion. "Next batter up!" he called hoarsely and sat down on the bench. He was breathing hard, and beads of sweat stood out on his brow.

Ken went up to Worry, feeling that now was the time to acquaint the coach with his new idea. Eager as Ken was, he had to force himself to take this step. All the hope and dread, nervousness and determination of the weeks of practice seemed to accumulate in that moment. He stammered and stuttered, grew speechless, and then as Worry looked up in kind surprise, Ken suddenly grew cool and earnest.

"Mr. Arthurs, will you try me in the box?"

"What's that, Peg?" queried the coach, sharply.

"Will you give me a trial in the box? I've wanted one all along. You put me in once when we were in the cage, but you made me hit the batters."

"Pitch? You, Peg? Why not? Why didn't I think of it? I'm sure gettin' to be like 'em fathead directors. You've got steam, Peg, but can you curve a ball? Let's see your fingers."

"Yes, I can curve a ball around a corner. Please give me a trial, Mr. Arthurs. I failed in the infield, and I'm little good in the outfield. But I know I can pitch."

The coach gave Ken one searching glance. Then he called all the candidates in to the plate, and ordered Dean, the stocky little catcher, to don his chest protector, mask, and mitt.

"Peg," said the coach, "Dean will signal you—

one finger for a straight ball, two for a curve."

When Ken walked to the box all his muscles seemed quivering and tense, and he had a contraction in his throat. This was his opportunity. He was not unnerved as he had been when he was trying for the other positions. All Ken's life he had been accustomed to throwing. At his home he had been the only boy who could throw a stone across the river, the only one who could get a ball over the high school tower. A favorite pastime had always been the throwing of small apples, or walnuts, or stones, and he had acquired an accuracy that made it futile for his boy comrades to compete with him. Curving a ball had come natural to him, and he would have pitched all his high school games had it not been for the fact that no one could catch him, and, moreover, none of the boys had found any fun in batting against him.

When Ken faced the first batter a feeling came over him that he had never before had on the ballfield. He was hot, trembling, hurried, but this new feeling was apart from these. His feet were on solid ground, and his arm felt as it always had in those throwing contests where he had so easily won. He seemed to decide from McCord's position at the plate what to throw him.

Ken took his swing. It was slow, easy, natural. But the ball traveled with much greater speed than the batter expected from such motion. McCord let the first two balls go by, and Arthurs called them both strikes. Then Ken pitched a curve which McCord fanned at helplessly. Arthurs sent Trace up next. Ken saw that the coach was sending up the weaker hitters first. Trace could not even make a foul. Raymond was third up, and Ken had to smile at the scowling second baseman. Remembering his weakness for pulling away from the plate, Ken threw Raymond two fast curves on the outside, and then a slow wide curve, far out. Raymond could not have hit the first two with a paddle, and the third lured him irresistibly out of position and made him look ridiculous. He slammed his bat down and slouched to the bench. Duncan turned out to be the next easy victim. Four batters had not so much as fouled Ken. And Ken knew he was holding himself in—that, in fact, he had not let out half his speed. Blake, the next player, hit up a little fly that Ken caught, and Schoonover made the fifth man to strike out.

Then Weir stood over the plate, and he was a short, sturdy batter, hard to pitch to. He looked as if he might be able to hit any kind of a ball. Ken tried him first with a straight fast one over the middle of the plate. Weir hit it hard, but it went foul. And through Ken's mind flashed the thought that he would pitch no more speed to Weir or players who swung as he did. Accordingly Ken tried the slow curve that had baffled Raymond. Weir popped it up and retired in disgust.

The following batter was Graves, who strode up smiling, confident, sarcastic, as if he knew he could do more than the others. Ken imagined what the third baseman would have said if the coach had not been present. Graves always ruffled Ken the wrong way.

"I'll strike him out if I break my arm!" muttered Ken to himself. He faced Graves deliberately and eyed his position at bat. Graves as deliberately laughed at him.

"Pitch up, pitch up!" he called out.

"Right over the pan!" retorted Ken, as quick as an echo. He went hot as fire all over. This fellow Graves had some strange power of infuriating him.

Ken took a different windup, which got more of his weight in motion, and let his arm out. Like a white bullet the ball shot plateward, rising a little so that Graves hit vainly under it. The ball surprised Dean, knocked his hands apart as if they had been paper, and resounded from his chest protector. Ken pitched the second ball in the same place with a like result, except that Dean held on to it. Graves had lost his smile and wore an expression of sickly surprise. The third ball traveled by him and cracked in Dean's mitt, and Arthurs called it a strike.

"Easy there—that'll do!" yelled the coach. "Come in here, Peg. Out on the field now, boys."

106

Homans stopped Ken as they were passing each other, and Ken felt himself under the scrutiny of clear gray eyes.

"Youngster, you look good to me," said Homans.

Ken also felt himself regarded with astonishment by many of the candidates; and Ray ran a keen, intuitive glance over him from head to foot. But it was the coach's manner that struck Ken most forcibly. Worry was utterly unlike himself.

"Why didn't you tell me about this before— you—you—" he yelled, red as a beet in the face. He grasped Ken with both hands, then he let him go, and picking up a ball and a mitt he grasped him again. Without a word he led Ken across the field and to a secluded corner behind the bleachers. Ken felt for all the world as if he was being led to execution.

Worry took off his coat and vest and collar. He arranged a block of wood for a plate and stepped off so many paces and placed another piece of wood to mark the pitcher's box. Then he donned the mitt.

"Peg, somethin's comin' off. I know it. I never make mistakes in sizin' up pitchers. But I've had such hard luck this season that I can't believe my own eyes. We've got to prove it. Now you go out there and pitch to me. Just natural-like at first."

Ken pitched a dozen balls or more, some screwballs, some curves. Then he threw what he called his drop, which he executed by a straight over-hand swing.

"Oh—a beauty!" yelled Worry. "Where, Peg, where did you learn that? Another, lower now."

Worry fell over trying to stop the glancing drop.

"Try straight ones now, Peg, right over the middle. See how many you can pitch."

One after another, with free, easy motion, Ken shot balls squarely over the plate. Worry counted them, and suddenly, after the fourteenth pitch, he stood up and glared at Ken.

"Are you goin' to keep puttin' 'em over this pan all day that way?"

"Mr. Arthurs, I couldn't miss that plate if I pitched a week," replied Ken.

"Stop callin' me Mister!" yelled Worry. "Now, put 'em where I hold my hands—inside corner . . . outside corner . . . again . . . inside now, low . . . another . . . a fast one over, now . . . high, in-side. Oh, Peg, this ain't right. I ain't seein' straight. I think I'm dreamin'. Come on with 'em!"

Fast and true Ken sped the balls into Worry's mitt. Seldom did the coach have to move his hands at all.

"Peg Ward, did you know that pitchin' was all control, putting' the ball where you wanted to?" asked Worry, stopping once more.

"No, I didn't," replied Ken.

"How did you learn to peg a ball as straight as this?"

Ken told him how he had thrown at marks all his life.

"Why didn't you tell me before?" Worry seemed not to be able to get over Ken's backwardness. "Look at the sleepless nights and the gray hairs you could have saved me." He stamped around as if furious, yet underneath the surface Ken saw that the coach was trying to hide his elation. "Here now," he shouted, suddenly, "a few more and *peg* 'em! See? Cut loose and let me see what steam you've got!"

Ken whirled with all his might and delivered the ball with all his weight. The ball seemed to diminish in size, it went so swiftly. Near the plate it took an upward jump, and it knocked Worry's mitt off his hand.

Worry yelled out; then he looked carefully at Ken, but he made no effort to go after the ball or pick up the mitt.

"Did I say for you to knock my block off? . . . Come here, Peg. You're only a youngster. Do you think you can keep that? Are you goin' to let me teach you to pitch? Have you got any nerve? Are you up in the air at the thought of Place and Herne?"

Then he actually hugged Ken and kept hold of him as if he might get away. He was panting and sweating. All at once he sat down on one of the braces of the bleachers and began mopping his face. He seemed to cool down, to undergo a subtle change.

"Peg," he said, quietly, "I'm as bad as some of 'em fathead directors. . . . You see I didn't have no kind of a pitcher to work on this spring. I kept on hopin'. Strange why I didn't quit. And now— my boy, you're a kid, but you're a natural-born pitcher."

· 11 ·

STATE UNIVERSITY GAME

ARTHURS returned to the diamond and called the squad around him. He might have been another coach from the change that was manifest in him.

"Boys, I've picked the varsity, and sorry I am to say you all can't be on it. Ward, Dean, McCord, Raymond, Weir, Graves, Ray, Homans, Trace, Duncan, and Schoonover—these men will report at once to trainer Murray and obey his orders. Then pack your trunks and report to me at 36 Spring Street tonight. That's all—up on your toes now. . . . The rest of you boys will each get his uniform and sweater, but, of course, I can't give you the varsity letter. You've all tried hard and done your best. I'm much obliged to you, and hope you'll try again next year."

Led by Arthurs, the players trotted across the field to Murray's quarters. Ken used all his eyes as he went in. This was the sacred precinct of the chosen athletes, and it was not open to any others. He saw a small gymnasium, and adjoining it a large, bright room with painted windows that let in the light, but could not be seen through. Around the room on two sides were arranged huge boxlike bins with holes in the lids and behind them along the wall were steam pipes. On the other two sides were little zinc-lined rooms, with different kinds of pipes, which Ken concluded were used for shower baths. Murray, the trainer, was there, and two lanky, grinning attendants with towels over their shoulders, and a little dried-up fellow who was all one smile.

"Murray, here's my bunch. Look 'em over, and tomorrow start 'em in for keeps," said Arthurs.

"Well, Worry, they're not a bad-looking lot. Slim and trim. We won't have to take off any beef. Here's Reddy Ray. I let you have him this year, Worry, but the track team will miss him. And here's Peg Ward. I was sure you'd pick him, Worry. And this is Homans, isn't it? I remember you in the freshmen games. The rest of you boys I'll have to get acquainted with. They say I'm a pretty hard fellow, but that's on the outside. Now, hustle out of your suits, and we'll give you all a good stew and a rubdown."

What the stew was soon appeared plain to Ken. He was the first player undressed, and Murray, lifting up one of the boxlids, pushed Ken inside.

"Sit down and put your feet in that pan," he directed. "When I drop the lid let your head come out the hole. There!" Then he wrapped a huge towel around Ken's neck, being careful to tuck it close and tight. With that he reached around to the back of the box and turned on the steam.

Ken felt like a jack-in-the-box. The warm steam was pleasant. He looked about him to see the other boys being placed in like positions. Raymond had the box on one side, and Reddy Ray the one on the other.

"It's great," said Ray, smiling at Ken. "You'll like it."

Raymond looked scared. Ken wondered if the fellow ever got any enjoyment out of things. Then Ken found himself attending to his own sensations. The steam was pouring out of the pipe inside the box, and it was growing wetter, thicker, and hotter. The pleasant warmth and tickling changed to a burning sensation. Ken found himself bathed in a heavy sweat. Then he began to smart in different places, and he was hard put to it to keep rubbing them. The steam grew hotter; his body was afire; his breath labored in great heaves. Ken felt that he must cry out. He heard exclamations, then yells, from some of the other boxed-up players, and he glanced quickly around. Reddy Ray was smiling, and did not look at all uncomfortable. But Raymond was scarlet in the face, and he squirmed his head to and fro.

"*Ough!*" he bawled. "Let me out of here!"

One of the attendants lifted the lid and helped

Raymond out. He danced about as if on hot bricks. His body was the color of a boiled lobster. The attendant put him under one of the showers and turned the water on. Raymond uttered one deep, low, "O-o-o-o!" Then McCord begged to be let out; Weir's big head, with its shock of hair, resembled that of an angry lion; little Trace screamed, and Duncan yelled.

"Peg, how're you?" asked Murray, walking up to Ken. "It's always pretty hot the first few times. But afterward it's fine. Look at Reddy."

"Murray, give Peg a good stewin'," put in Arthurs. "He's got a great arm, and we must take care of it."

Ken saw the other boys, except Ray, let out, and he simply could not endure the steam any longer.

"I've got—enough," he stammered.

"Scotty, turn on a little more stew," ordered Murray, cheerfully; then he rubbed his hand over Ken's face. "You're not hot yet!"

Scotty turned on more steam, and Ken felt it as a wet flame. He was being flayed alive.

"Please—please—let me out!" he implored.

With a laugh Murray lifted the lid, and Ken hopped out. He was as red as anything red he had ever seen. Then Scotty shoved him under a shower, and as the icy water came down in a deluge Ken lost his breath, his chest caved in, and he gasped. Scotty led him out into the room, dried him with a towel, rubbed him down, and then, resting Ken's arm on his shoulder, began to pat and beat and massage it. In a few moments Ken thought his arm was a piece of live India rubber. He had never been in such a glow. When he had dressed he felt as light as air, strong, fresh, and keen for action.

"Hustle now, Peg," said Arthurs. "Get your things packed. Supper tonight at the trainin' house."

It was after dark when Ken got an expressman to haul his trunk to the address on Spring Street. The house was situated about the middle of a four-storied block, and within sight of Grant Field. Worry answered his ring.

"Here you are, Peg, the last one. I was beginnin' to worry about you. Have your trunk taken right up, third floor back. Hurry down, for dinner will be ready soon."

Ken followed at the heels of the expressman up to his room. He was surprised and somewhat taken aback to find Raymond sitting upon the bed.

"Hello! excuse me," said Ken. "Guess I've got the wrong place."

"The coach said you and I were to room together," returned Raymond.

"Us? Roommates?" ejaculated Ken.

Raymond took offense at this.

"Wull, I guess I can stand it," he growled.

"I hope I can," was Ken's short reply. It was Ken's failing that he could not help retaliating. But he was also as repentant as he was quick-tempered. "Oh, I didn't mean that. . . . See here, Raymond, if we've got to be roommates—" Ken paused in embarrassment.

"Wull, we're both on the varsity," said Raymond.

"That's so," rejoined Ken, brightening. "It makes a whole lot of difference, doesn't it?"

Raymond got off the bed and looked at Ken.

"What's your first name?" queried he. "I don't like 'Peg.' "

"Kenneth. Ken, for short. What's yours?"

"Mine's Kel. Wull, Ken—"

Having gotten so far Raymond hesitated, and it was Ken who first offered his hand. Raymond eagerly grasped it. That broke the ice.

"Kel, I haven't liked your looks at all," said Ken apologetically.

"Ken, I've been going to lick you all spring."

They went downstairs arm in arm.

It was with great interest and curiosity that Ken looked about the cozy and comfortable rooms. The walls were adorned with pictures of varsity teams and players, and the college colors were much in evidence. College magazines and papers littered the table in the reading room.

"Boys, we'll be pretty snug and nice here when things get to runnin' smooth. The grub will be plain, but there's plenty of it."

There were twelve in all at the table, with the coach seated at the head. The boys were hungry, and besides, as they had as yet had no chance to become acquainted, the conversation lagged. The newness and strangeness, however, did not hide the general air of suppressed gratification. After dinner Worry called them all together in the reading room.

"Well, boys, here we are together like one big family, and we're shut in for two months. Now, I know you've all been fightin' for places on the team, and have had no chance to be friendly. It's always that way in the beginnin', and I dare say there'll be some scraps among you before things straighten out. We'll have more to say about that later. The thing now is you're all varsity men, and I'm puttin' you on your word of honor. Your word is good enough for me. Here's my rules, and I'm more than usually particular this year, for reasons I'll tell later.

"You're not to break trainin'. You're not to eat anything anywhere but here. You're to cut out cigarettes and drinks. You're to be in bed at ten o'clock. And I advise, although I ain't insistin', that if you have any leisure time you'll spend most of it here. That's all."

117

For Ken the three days following passed as so many hours. He did not in the least dread the approaching game with State University, but his mind held scarcely anything outside of Arthurs' coaching. The practice of the players had been wholly different. It was as if they had been freed from some binding spell. Worry kept them at fielding and batting for four full hours every afternoon. Ken, after pitching to Dean for a while, batted to the infield and so had opportunity to see the improvement. Graves was brilliant at third, Weir was steady and sure at short, Raymond seemed to have springs in his legs and pounced upon the ball with wonderful quickness, and McCord fielded all his chances successfully.

On the afternoon of the game Worry waited at the training house until all the players came downstairs in uniform.

"Boys, what's happened in the past doesn't count. We start over today. I'm not goin' to say much or confuse you with complex team coachin'. But I'm hopeful. I sort of think there's a rabbit in our hats. I'll tell you tonight if I'm right. Think of how you have been roasted by the students. Play like tigers. Put out of your mind everything but tryin'. Nothin' counts for you, boys. Errors are nothin'; mistakes are nothin'. Play the game as one man. Don't think of yourselves. You all know when you ought to hit or bunt or run. I'm trustin' you. I won't say a word from the bench.

118

And don't underrate our chances. Remember that I think it's possible we may have somethin' up our sleeves. That's all from me till after the game."

Worry walked to Grant Field with Ken. He talked as they went along, but not on baseball. The State team was already out and practicing. Worry kept Ken near him on the bench and closely watched the visitors in practice. When the gong rang to call them in he sent his players out, with a remark to Ken to take his warm-up easily. Ken thought he had hardly warmed up at all before the coach called him in.

"Peg, listen!" he whispered. His gaze seemed to hypnotize Ken. "Do you have any idea what you'll do to this bunch from State?"

"Why—no—I—"

"Listen! I tell you I know they won't be able to touch you. . . . Size up batters in your own way. If they look as if they'd pull or chop on a curve, hand it up. If not, peg 'em a straight one over the inside corner, high. If you get in a hole with runners on bases use that fast jump ball, as hard as you can drive it, right over the pan. . . . Go in with perfect confidence. I wouldn't say that to you, Peg, if I didn't feel it myself, honestly. I'd say for you to do your best. But I've sized up these State fellows, and they won't be able to touch you. Remember what I say. That's all."

"I'll remember," said Ken, soberly.

When the umpire called the game there were perhaps fifty students in the bleachers and a few spectators in the grandstand, so poor an attendance that the State players loudly voiced their derision.

"Hey! boys," yelled one, "we drew a crowd last year, and look at that!"

"It's Wayne's dub team," replied another. They ran upon the field as if the result of the game was a foregone conclusion. Their pitcher, a lanky individual, handled the ball with assurance.

Homans led off for Wayne. He stood left-handed at the plate, and held his bat almost in the middle. He did not swing, but poked at the first ball pitched and placed a short hit over third. Raymond, also left-handed, came next, and, letting two balls go, he bunted the third. Running fast, he slid into first base and beat the throw. Homans kept swiftly on toward third, drew the throw, and, sliding, was also safe. It was fast work, and the Wayne players seemed to rise off the bench with the significance of the play. Worry Arthurs looked on from under the brim of his hat and spoke no word. Then Reddy Ray stepped up.

"They're all left-handed!" shouted a State player. The pitcher looked at Reddy, then motioned for his outfielders to play deeper. With that he delivered the ball, which the umpire called a strike. Reddy stood still and straight while two more balls sped by; then he swung on the next. A vicious low hit cut out over first base and skipped in great bounds to the fence. Homans scored. Raymond turned at second, going fast. But it was Ray's speed that electrified the watching players. They jumped up cheering.

"Oh, see him run!" yelled Ken.

He was on third before Raymond reached the plate. Weir lifted a high fly to left field, and when the ball dropped into the fielder's hands Ray ran home on the throw-in. Three runs had been scored in a twinkling. It amazed the State team. They were not slow in bandying remarks among themselves. "Fast! Who's that redhead? Is this your dub team? Get in the game, boys!" They began to think more of playing ball and less of their own superiority. Graves, however, and McCord following him, went out upon plays to the infield.

As Ken walked out toward the pitcher's box Homans put a hand on his arm, and said: "Kid, put them all over. Don't waste any. Make every batter hit. Keep your nerve. We're back of you out here." Then Reddy Ray, in passing, spoke with a cool, quiet faith that thrilled Ken, "Peg, we've got enough runs now to win."

Ken faced the plate all in a white glow. He was far from calmness, but it was a restless, fiery hurry for the action of the game. He remembered the look in Worry's eyes, and every word that he had spoken rang in his ears. Receiving the ball from

121

the umpire, he stepped upon the slab with a sudden, strange, deep tremor. It passed as quickly, and then he was eyeing the first batter. He drew a long breath, standing motionless, with all the significance of Worry's hope flashing before him, and then he whirled and delivered the ball. The batter struck at it after it had passed him, and it cracked in Dean's mitt.

"Speed!" called the State captain. "Quick eye, there!"

The batter growled some unintelligible reply. Then he fouled the second ball, missed the next, and was out. The succeeding State player hit an easy fly to Homans, and the next had two strikes called upon him and swung vainly at the third.

Dean got a base on balls for Wayne, Trace went out trying to bunt, and Ken hit to short, forcing Dean at second. Homans lined to third, retiring the side. The best that the State players could do in their half was for one man to send a weak grounder to Raymond, one to fly out, and the other to fail on strikes. Wayne went to bat again, and Raymond got his base by being hit by a pitched ball. Reddy Ray bunted and was safe. Weir struck out. Graves rapped a safety through short, scoring Raymond, and sending Ray to third. Then McCord fouled out to the catcher. Again, in State's inning, they failed to get on base, being unable to hit Ken effectively.

So the game progressed, State slowly losing its

aggressive playing, and Wayne gaining what its opponents had lost. In the sixth Homans reached his base on an error, stole second, went to third on Raymond's sacrifice, and scored on Reddy's drive to right. State flashed up in their half, getting two men to first on misplays of McCord and Weir, and scored a run on a slow hit to Graves.

With the bases full, Ken let his arm out and pitched the fastball at the limit of his speed. The State batters were helpless before it, but they scored two runs on passed balls by Dean. The little catcher had a hard time judging Ken's rising fastball. That ended the run getting for State, though they came near scoring again on more fumbling in the infield. In the eighth Ken landed a safe fly over second, and tallied on a double by Homans.

Before Ken knew the game was half over it had ended—Wayne 6, State 3. His players crowded around him and someone called for the Wayne yell. It was given with wild vehemence.

From that moment until dinner was over at the training house Ken appeared to be the center of a humming circle. What was said and done he never remembered. Then the coach stopped the excitement.

"Boys, now for a heart-to-heart talk," he said, with a smile both happy and grave. "We won today, as I predicted. State had a fairly strong team, but if Ward had received perfect support they would not have got a man beyond second. That's the only personal mention I'll make. Now, listen. . . ."

He paused, with his eyes glinting brightly and his jaw quivering.

"I expected to win, but before the game I never dreamed of our possibilities. I got a glimpse now of what hard work and a demon spirit to play together might make of this team. I've had an inspiration. We are goin' to beat Herne and play Place to a standstill."

Not a boy moved an eyelash as Arthurs made this statement, and the sound of a pin dropping could have been heard.

"To do that we must pull together as no boys ever pulled together before. We must be all one heart. We must be actuated by one spirit. Listen! If you will stick together and to me, I'll make a team that will be a wonder. Never the hittin' team as good as last year's varsity, but a faster team, a finer machine. Think of that! Think of how we have been treated this year! For that we'll win all the greater glory. It's worth all there is in you, boys. You would have the proudest record of any team that ever played for old Wayne.

"I love the old college, boys, and I've given it the best years of my life. If it's anything to you, why, understand that if I fail to build up a good team this year I shall be let go by those directors who have made the change in athletics. I could

stand that, but—I've a boy of my own who's pre-
parin' for Wayne, and my heart is set on seein'
him enter—and he said he never will if they let
me go. So, you youngsters and me—we've much
to gain. Go to your rooms now and think, think
as you never did before, until the spirit of this
thing, the possibility of it, grips you as it has me."

· 12 ·

KEN CLASHES WITH GRAVES

Two weeks after the contest with State University four more games with minor colleges had been played and won by Wayne. Hour by hour the coach had drilled the players; day by day the grilling practice told in their quickening grasp of team play, in the gradual correction of erratic fielding and wild throwing. Every game a few more students attended, reluctantly, in a half-hearted manner.

"We're comin' with a rush," said Worry to Ken. "Say, but Dale and the old gang have a surprise in store for 'em! And the students—they're goin' to drop dead pretty soon . . . Peg, Murray tells me he's puttin' weight on you."

"Why, yes, it's the funniest thing," replied Ken. "Today I weighed one hundred and sixty-four. Worry, I'm afraid I'm getting fat."

"Fat, nothin'," snorted Worry. "It's muscle. I told Murray to put beef on you all he can. Pretty soon you'll be able to peg a ball through the back-stop. Dean's too light, Peg. He's plucky and will

126

make a catcher, but he's too light. You're batterin' him all up."

Worry shook his head seriously.

"Oh, he's fine!" exclaimed Ken. "I'm not afraid anymore. He digs my drop out of the dust, and I can't get a curve away from him. He's weak only on the jump ball, and I don't throw that often, only when I let drive."

"You'll be usin' that often enough against Herne and Place. I'm dependin' on that for those games. Peg, are you worryin' any, losin' any sleep, over those games?"

"Indeed I'm not," replied Ken, laughing.

"Say, I wish you'd have a balloon ascension, and have it quick. It ain't natural, Peg, for you not to get a case of rattles. It's comin' to you, and I don't want it in any of the big games."

"I don't want it either. But Worry, pitching is all a matter of control, you say so often. I don't believe I could get wild and lose my control if I tried."

"Peg, you sure have the best control of any pitcher I ever coached. It's your success. It'll make a great pitcher out of you. All you've got to learn is where to pitch 'em to Herne and Place."

"How am I to learn that?"

"Listen!" Worry whispered. "I'm goin' to send you to Washington next week to see Place and Herne play Georgetown. You'll pay your little money and sit in the grandstand right behind the catcher. You'll have a pencil and a scorecard, and you'll be enjoyin' the game. But, Peg, you'll also be usin' your head, and when you see one of 'em players pull away on a curve, or hit weak on a sinker, or miss a high fast one, or slug a low ball, you will jot it down on your card. You'll watch Place's hard hitters with hawk eyes, my boy, and a pitcher's memory. And when they come along to Grant Field you'll have 'em pretty well sized up."

"That's fine, Worry, but is it fair?" queried Ken.

"Fair? Why, of course. They all do it. We saw Place's captain in the grandstand here last spring."

The coach made no secret of his pride and faith in Ken. It was this, perhaps, as much as anything, which kept Ken keyed up. For Ken was really pitching better ball than he knew how to pitch. He would have broken his arm for Worry; he believed absolutely in what the coach told him; he did not think of himself at all.

Worry, however, had plenty of enthusiasm for his other players. Every evening after dinner he would call them all about him and talk for an hour. Sometimes he would tell funny baseball stories; again, he told of famous Wayne–Place games, and how they had been won or lost; then at other times he dwelt on the merits and faults of his own team. In speaking of the swift development of this year's varsity he said it was as remarkable as it had been unforeseen. He claimed it would be a bewildering surprise to Wayne students and to the big college teams. He was working toward the perfection of a fast run-getting machine. In the five games already played and won a good idea could be gotten of Wayne's team, individually and collectively. Homans was a scientific short-field hitter and remarkably sure. Raymond could not bat, but he had developed into a wonder in reaching first base, by bunt or base on balls, or being hit. Reddy Ray was a hard and timely batter, and when he got on base his wonderful fleetness made him almost sure to score. Of the other players Graves batted the best; but taking the team as a whole, and comparing them with Place or Herne, it appeared that Reddy and Homans were the only great hitters, and the two of them, of course, could not make a great hitting team. In fielding, however, the coach said he had never seen the like. They were all fast, and Homans was perfect in judgment on fly balls, and Raymond was quick as lightning to knock down base hits, and as for the intercollegiate sprinter in left field, it was simply a breathtaking event to see him run after a ball. Last of all was Ken Ward with his great arm. It was a strangely assorted team, Worry said, one impossible to judge at the moment, but it was one to watch.

"Boys, we're comin' with a rush," he went on to say. "But somethin's holdin' us back a little.

There's no lack of harmony, yet there's a drag. In spite of the spirit you've shown—and I want to say it's been great—the team doesn't work together as one man *all* the time. I advise you all to stick closer together. Stay away from the club, and everywhere except lectures. We've got to be closer'n brothers. It'll all work out right before we go up against Herne in June. That game's comin', boys, and by that time the old college will be crazy. It'll be *our* turn then."

Worry's talks always sank deeply into Ken's mind and set him to thinking and revolving over and over the gist of them so that he could remember to his profit.

He knew that some the boys had broken training, and he pondered if that was what caused the drag Worry mentioned. Ken had come to feel the life and fortunes of the varsity so keenly that he realized how the simplest deviations from honor might affect the smooth running of the team. It must be perfectly smooth. And to make it so every player must be of one mind.

Ken proved to himself how lack of the highest spirit on the part of one or two of the team tended toward the lowering of the general spirit. For he began to worry, and almost at once it influenced his playing. He found himself growing watchful of his comrades and fearful of what they might be doing. He caught himself being ashamed of his suspicions. He would have preferred to cut off his hand rather than break his promise to the coach. Perhaps, however, he exaggerated his feeling and sense of duty. He remembered the scene in Dale's room the night he refused to smoke and drink; how Dale had commended his refusal. Nevertheless, he gathered from Dale's remark to Worry that breaking training was not unusual or particularly harmful.

"With Dale's team it might not have been so bad," thought Ken. "But it's different with us. We've got to make up in spirit what we lack in ability."

Weir and McCord occupied the room next to Ken's, and Graves and Trace, rooming together, were also on that floor. Ken had tried with all his might to feel friendly toward the third baseman. He had caught Graves carrying cake and pie to his room and smoking cigarettes with the window open. One night Graves took cigarettes from his pocket and offered them to Kel, Trace, and Ken, who all happened to be in Ken's room at the time. Trace readily accepted; Kel demurred at first, but finally took one. Graves then tossed the pack to Ken.

"No, I don't smoke. Besides, it's breaking training," said Ken.

"You make me sick, Ward," retorted Graves. "You're a wet blanket. Do you think we're going to be as sissy as that? It's hard enough to stand the grub we get here, without giving up a little smoke."

Ken made no reply, but he found it difficult to smother a hot riot in his breast. When the other boys had gone to their rooms Ken took Kel to task about his wrong-doing.

"Do you think that's the right sort of thing? What would Worry say?"

"Ken, I don't care about it, not a bit," replied Kel, flinging his cigarette out of the window. "But Graves is always asking me to do things—I hate to refuse. It seems so—"

"Kel, if Worry finds it out you'll lose your place on the team."

"No!" exclaimed Raymond, staring.

"Mark what I say. I wish you'd stop letting Graves coax you into things."

"Ken, he's always smuggling pie and cake and candy into his room. I've had some of it. Trace said he'd brought in something to drink, too."

"It's a shame," cried Ken, in anger. "I never liked him and I've tried hard to change it. Now I'm glad I couldn't."

"He doesn't have any use for you," replied Kel. "He's always running you down to the other boys. What'd you ever do to him, Ken?"

"Oh, it was that potato stunt of mine last fall. He's a Soph, and I hit him, I guess."

"I think it's more than that," went on Raymond.

"Anyway, you look out for him, because he's aching to spoil your face."

"He is, is he?" snapped Ken.

Ken was too angry to talk anymore, and so the boys went to bed. The next few days Ken discovered that either out of shame or growing estrangement Raymond avoided him, and he was bitterly hurt. He had come to like the little second baseman and had hoped they would be good friends. It was easy to see that Graves became daily bolder, and more lax in training, and his influence upon several of the boys grew stronger. And when Dean, Schoonover, and Duncan appeared to be joining the clique, Ken decided he would have to talk to someone, so he went up to see Ray and Homans.

The sprinter was alone, sitting by his lamp, with books and notes spread before him.

"Hello, Peg! come in. You look a little glum. What's wrong?"

Reddy Ray seemed like an elder brother to Ken, and he found himself blurting out his trouble. Ray looked thoughtful, and after a moment he replied in his quiet way:

"Peg, it's new to you, but it's an old story to me. The track and crew men seldom break training, which is more than can be said of the other athletes. It seems to me baseball fellows are the most careless. They really don't have to train so conscientiously. It's only a kind of form."

"But it's different this year," burst out Ken. "You know what Worry said, and how he trusts us."

"You're right, Peg, only you mustn't take it so hard. Things will work out all right. Homans and I were talking about that today. You see, Worry wants the boys to elect a captain soon. But perhaps he has not confided in you youngsters. He will suggest that you elect Homans or me. Well, I won't run for the place, so it'll be Homans. He's the man to captain us, that's certain. Graves thinks, though, that he can pull the wires and be elected captain. He's way off. Besides, Peg, he's making a big mistake. Worry doesn't like him, and when he finds out about this break in training we'll have a new third baseman. No doubt Blake will play the bag. Graves is the only drag in Worry's baseball machine now, and he'll not last. . . . So, Peg, don't think anymore about it. Mind you, the whole team circles around you. You're the pivot, and as sure as you're born you'll be Wayne's captain next year. That's something for you to keep in mind and work for. If Graves keeps after you—hand him one! That's not against rules. Punch him! If Worry knew the truth he would pat you on the back for slugging Graves. Cheer up, Peg! Even if Graves has got all the kids on his side, which I doubt, Homans and I are with you. And you can just bet that Worry Arthurs will side with us. . . . Now run along, for I must study."

This conversation was most illuminating to Ken. He left Reddy's room all in a quiver of warm pleasure and friendliness at the great sprinter's quiet praise and advice. To make such a friend was worth losing a hundred friends like Graves. He dismissed the third baseman and his scheming from mind, and believed Reddy as he had believed Arthurs. But Ken thought much of what he divined was a glimmering of the inside workings of a college baseball team. He had one wild start of rapture at the idea of becoming captain of Wayne's varsity next year, and then he dared think no more of that.

The day dawned for Ken to go to Washington, and he was so perturbed at his responsibilities that he quite forgot to worry about the game Wayne had to play in his absence. Arthurs intended to pitch Schoonover in that game, and had no doubt as to its outcome. The coach went to the station with Ken, once more repeated his instructions, and saw him upon the train. Certainly there was no more important personage on board that Washington Limited than Ken Ward. In fact, Ken was so full of importance and responsibility that he quite divided his time between foolish pride in his being chosen to "size up" the great college teams and fearful conjecture as to his ability.

At any rate, the time flew by, the trip seemed short, and soon he was on the Georgetown field. It was lucky that he arrived early and got a seat in the middle of the grandstand, for there was a throng in attendance when the players came on the diamond. The noisy bleachers, the merry laughter, the flashing colors, and especially the bright gowns and pretty faces of the girls gave Ken pleasurable consciousness of what it would mean to play before such a crowd. At Wayne he had pitched to empty seats. Remembering Worry's prophecy, however, he was content to wait.

From that moment his duty absorbed him. He found it exceedingly fascinating to study the batters, and utterly forgot his responsibility. Not only did he jot down on his card his idea of the weakness and strength of the different hitters, but he compared what he would have pitched to them with what was actually pitched. Of course, he had no test of his comparison, but he felt intuitively that he had the better of it. Watching so closely, Ken had forced home to him Arthurs' repeated assertion that control of the ball made a pitcher. Both pitchers in this game were wild. Locating the plate with them was more a matter of luck than ability. The Herne pitcher kept wasting balls and getting himself in the hole, and then the heavy Georgetown players would know when he had to throw a strike, if he could, and accordingly they hit hard. They beat Herne badly.

The next day in the game with Place it was a different story. Ken realized he was watching a great team. They reminded him of Dale's varsity, though they did not play that fiendish right-field-hitting game. Ken felt a numbness come over him at the idea of facing this Place team. It soon passed, for they had their vulnerable places. It was not so much that they hit hard on speed and curves, for they got them where they wanted them. Keene flied out on high fastballs over the inside corner; Starke bit at low drops; Martin was weak on a slowball; MacNeff, the captain, could not touch speed under his chin, and he always struck at it. On the other hand, he killed a low ball. Prince was the only man who, in Ken's judgment, seemed to have no weakness. These men represented the batting strength of Place, and Ken, though he did not in the least underestimate them, had no fear. He would have liked to pitch against them right there.

"It's all in control of the ball," thought Ken. "Here are seventeen bases on balls in two games—four pitchers. They're wild. . . . But suppose I got wild, too?"

The idea made Ken shiver.

He traveled all night, sleeping on the train, and got home to the training house about nine the next morning. Worry was out, Scotty said, and the boys had all gone over to college. Ken went upstairs and found Raymond in bed.

"Why, Kel, what's the matter?" asked Ken.

"I'm sick," replied Kel. He was pale and appeared to be in distress.

"Oh, I'm sorry. Can't I do something? Get you some medicine? Call Murray?"

"Ken, don't call anybody, unless you want to see me disgraced. Worry got out this morning before he noticed my absence from breakfast. I was scared to death."

"Scared? Disgraced?"

"Ken, I drank a little last night. It always makes me sick. You know I've a weak stomach."

"Kel, you didn't drink, *say* you didn't!" implored Ken, sitting miserably down on the bed.

"Yes, I did. I believe I was half drunk. I can't stand anything. I'm sick, sick of myself, too, this morning. And I hate Graves."

Ken jumped up with kindling eyes.

"Kel, you've gone back on me—we'd started to be such friends—I tried to persuade you—"

"I know. I'm sorry, Ken. But I really liked you best. I was—you know how it is, Ken. If only Worry don't find it out!"

"Tell him," said Ken, quickly.

"What?" groaned Kel, in fright.

"Tell him. Let me tell him for you."

"No—no—no. He'd fire me off the team, and I couldn't stand that."

"I'll bet Worry wouldn't do anything of the kind. Maybe he knows more than you think."

"I'm afraid to tell him, Ken. I just can't tell him."

"But you gave your word of honor not to break training. The only thing left is to confess."

"I won't tell, Ken. It's not so much my own place on the team—there are the other fellows."

Ken saw that it was no use to argue with Raymond while he was so sick and discouraged, so he wisely left off talking and did his best to make him comfortable. Raymond dropped asleep after a little, and when he awakened just before lunchtime he appeared better.

"I won't be able to practice today," he said, "but I'll go down to lunch."

As he was dressing the boys began to come in from college and ran whistling up the stairs.

Graves bustled into the room with rather anxious haste.

"How're you feeling?" he asked.

"Pretty rocky. Graves—I told Ward about it," said Raymond.

Upon his hurried entrance Graves had not observed Ken.

"What did you want to do that for?" he demanded arrogantly.

Raymond looked at him, but made no reply.

"Ward, I suppose you'll squeal," said Graves, sneeringly. "That'll about be your speed."

Ken rose and, not trusting himself to speak, remained silent.

"You sissy!" cried Graves hotly. "Will you peach on us to Arthurs?"

"No. But if you don't get out of my room I'll hand you one," replied Ken, his voice growing thick.

Graves's face became red as fire.

"What? Why, you white-faced, white-haired freshman! I've been aching to punch you!"

"Well, why don't you commence?"

With the first retort Ken had felt a hot trembling go over him, and having yielded to his anger he did not care what happened.

"Ken—Graves," pleaded Raymond, white as a sheet. "Don't—please!" He turned from one to the other. "Don't scrap!"

"Graves, it's up to someone to call you, and I'm going to do it," said Ken passionately. "You've been after me all season, but I wouldn't care about that. It's your rotten influence on Kel and the other boys that makes me wild. You are the drag in this baseball team. You are a crack ballplayer, but you don't know what college spirit means. You're a mucker!"

"I'll lick you for that!" raved Graves, shaking his fists.

"You can't lick me!"

"Come outdoors. I dare you to come outdoors. I dare you!"

Ken strode out of the room and started down

the hall. "Come on!" he called grimly and ran down the stairs. Graves hesitated a moment, then followed.

Raymond suddenly called after them:

"Give it to him, Ken! Slug him! Beat him all up!"

· 13 ·

FRIENDSHIP

A HALF HOUR or less afterward Ken entered the
training house. It chanced that the boys, having
come in, were at the moment passing through the
hall to the dining room, and with them was Worry
Arthurs.

"Hello! you back? What's the matter with you?"
demanded the coach.

Ken's lips were puffed and bleeding, and his
chin was bloody. Sundry red and dark marks dis-
figured his usually clear complexion. His eyes
were blazing, and his hair rumpled down over his
brow.

"You've been in a scrap," declared Worry.

"I know it," said Ken. "Let me go up and wash."

Worry had planted himself at the foot of the
stairway in front of Ken. The boys stood silent
and aghast. Suddenly there came thumps upon
the stairs, and Raymond appeared, jumping down
three steps at a time. He dodged under Worry's
arm and plunged at Ken to hold him with both
hands.

"Ken! You're all bloody!" he exclaimed in great excitement. "He didn't lick you? Say he didn't! He's got to fight me, too! You're all messed up!"

"Wait till you see him!" muttered Ken.

"A-huh!" said Worry. "Been scrappin' with Graves! What for?"

"It's a personal matter," replied Ken.

"Come on, no monkey biz with me," said the coach, sharply. "Out with it!"

There was a moment's silence.

"Mr. Arthurs, it's my fault," burst out Raymond, flushed and eager. "Ken was fighting on my account."

"It wasn't anything of the kind," retorted Ken vehemently.

"Yes it was," cried Raymond, "and I'm going to tell why."

The hall door opened to admit Graves. He was disheveled, dirty, battered, and covered with blood. When he saw the group in the hall he made as if to dodge out.

"Here, come on! Take your medicine," called Worry tersely.

Graves shuffled in, cast down and sheepish, a very different fellow from his usual vaunting self.

"Now, Raymond, what's this all about?" demanded Worry.

Raymond changed color, but he did not hesitate an instant.

"Ken came in this morning and found me sick

143

in bed. I told him I had been half drunk last night—and that Graves had gotten me to drink. Then Graves came in. He and Ken had hard words. They went outdoors to fight."

"Would you have told me?" roared the coach in fury. "Would you have come to me with this if I hadn't caught Peg?"

Raymond faced him without flinching.

"At first I thought not—when Ken begged me to confess I just couldn't. But now I know I would."

At that Worry lost his sudden heat, and then he turned to the stricken Graves.

"Mebbe it'll surprise you, Graves, to learn that I knew a little of what you've been doin'. I told Homans to go to you in a quiet way and tip off your mistake. I hoped you'd see it. But you didn't. Then you've been knockin' Ward all season, for no reason I could discover but jealousy. Now, listen! Peg Ward has done a lot for me already this year, and he'll do more. But even if he beats Place, it won't mean any more to me than the beatin' he's given you. Now, you pack your things and get out of here. There's no position for you on this varsity."

Without a word in reply and amid intense silence, Graves went slowly upstairs. When he disappeared Worry sank into a chair, and looked as if he was about to collapse. Little Trace walked

hesitatingly forward with the manner of one pro-
pelled against his will.

"Mr. Arthurs, I—I," he stammered "—I'm
guilty, too. I broke training. I want to—"

The coach waved him back. "I don't want to
hear it, not another word—from anybody. It's
made me sick. I can't stand anymore. Only I see
I've got to change my rules. There won't be any
rules anymore. You can all do as you like. I'd
rather have you all go stale than practice deceit
on me. I cut out the trainin' rules."

"*No!*" The team rose up as one man and flung
the refusal at the coach.

"Worry, we won't stand for that," spoke up
Reddy Ray. His smooth, cool voice was like oil
on troubled waters. "I think Homans and I can
answer for the kids from now on. Graves was a
disorganizer-—that's the least I'll say of him. We'll
elect Homans captain of the team, and then we'll
cut loose like a lot of demons. It's been a long,
hard drill for you, Worry, but we're in the stretch
now and going to finish fast. We've been a kind
of misfit team all spring. You've had a blind faith
that something could be made out of us. Homans
has waked up to our hidden strength. And I go
further than that. I've played ball for years. I know
the game. I held down left field for two seasons
on the greatest college team ever developed out
West. That's new to you. Well, it gives me license

to talk a little. I want to tell you that I can *feel* what's in this team. It's like the feeling I have when I'm running against a fast man in the sprints. From now on we'll be a family of brothers with one idea. And that'll be to play Place off their feet."

Coach Arthurs sat up as if he had been given the elixir of life. Likewise the members of the team appeared to be under the spell of a powerful stimulus. The sprinter's words struck fire from all present.

Homans's clear gray eyes were like live coals. "Boys! One rousing cheer for Worry Arthurs and for Wayne!"

Lusty, strained throats let out the cheer with a deafening roar.

It was strange and significant at that moment to see Graves, white-faced and sullen, come down the stairs and pass through the hall and out of the door. It was as if discord, selfishness, and wavering passed out with him. Arthurs and Homans and Ray could not have hoped for a more striking lesson to the young players.

Dave, the waiter, appeared in the doorway of the dining room. "Mr. Arthurs, I called you all to lunch ten minutes ago. Lunch is gittin' cold."

That afternoon Wayne played the strong Hornell University nine.

Blake, new at third base for Wayne, was a revelation. He was all legs and arms. Weir accepted

146

eight chances. Raymond, sick or not, was all over
the infield, knocking down grounders, backing up
every play. To McCord, balls in the air or at his
feet were all the same. Trace caught a foul fly
right off the bleachers. Homans fielded with as
much speed as the old varsity's center and with
better judgment. Besides, he made four hits and
four runs. Reddy Ray drove one ball into the
bleachers, and on a line drive to left field he circled the bases in time that Murray said was wonderful. Dean stood up valiantly to his battering,
and for the first game had no passed balls. And
Ken Ward whirled tirelessly in the box, and one
after another he shot fast balls over the plate. He
made the Hornell players hit; he had no need to
extend himself to the use of the long swing and
whip of his arm that produced the rising fastball;
and he shut them out without a run, and gave
them only two safe hits. All through the game
Worry Arthurs sat on the bench without giving
an order or a sign. His worried look had vanished
with the crude playing of his team.

That night the Hornell captain, a veteran player
of unquestionable ability, was entertained at Carlton Hall by Wayne friends, and he expressed himself forcibly: "We came over to beat Wayne's weak
team. It'll be some time till we discover what
happened. Young Ward has the most magnificent
control and speed. He's absolutely relentless. And
that frog-legged second baseman—oh, say, can't

he cover ground! Homans is an all-around star. Then, your redheaded Ray, the sprinter—he's a marvel. Ward, Homans, Ray—they're demons, and they're making demons of the kids. I can't understand why Wayne students don't support their team. It's strange."

What the Hornell captain said went from lip to lip throughout the club, and then it spread, like a flame in windblown grass, from club to dormitory, and thus over all the university.

"Boys, the college is wakin' up," said Worry, rubbing his hands. "Yesterday's game jarred 'em. They can't believe their own ears. Why, Hornell almost beat Dale's team last spring. Now, kids, look out. We'll stand for no fussin' over us. We don't want any jollyin'. We've waited long for encouragement. It didn't come, and now we'll play out the string alone. There'll be a rush to Grant Field. It cuts no ice with us. Let 'em come to see the boys they hissed and mocked early in the spring. We'll show 'em a few things. We'll make 'em speechless. We'll make 'em so ashamed they won't know what to do. We'll repay all their slights by beatin' Place."

Worry was as excited as on the day he discovered that Ken was a pitcher.

"One more word, boys," he went on. "Keep together now. Run back here to your rooms as quick as you get leave from college. Be civil when you are approached by students, but don't mingle, not yet. Keep to yourselves. Your reward is comin'. It'll be great. Only wait!"

And that was the last touch of fire which molded Worry's players into a family of brothers. Close and warm and fine was the culmination of their friendship. On the field they were dominated by one impulse, almost savage in its intensity. When they were off the field the springs of youth burst forth to flood the hours with fun.

In the mornings when the mailman came there was always a wild scramble for letters. And it developed that Weir received more than his share. He got mail every day, and his good fortune could not escape the lynx eyes of his comrades. Nor could the size and shape of the envelope and the neat, small handwriting fail to be noticed. Weir always stole off by himself to read his daily letter, trying to escape a merry chorus of tantalizing remarks.

"Oh! Sugar!"

"Dreamy Eyes!"

"Gosh, the pink letter has come!"

Weir's reception of these sallies earned him the name of Puff.

One morning, for some unaccountable reason, Weir did not get downstairs when the mail arrived. Duncan got the pink letter, scrutinized the writing closely, and put the letter in his coat. Presently Weir came bustling down.

"Who's got the mail?" he asked quickly.

"No letters this morning," replied someone.

"Is this Sunday?" asked Weir, rather stupidly.

"Nope. I meant no letters for you."

Weir looked blank, then stunned, then crest-fallen. Duncan handed out the pink envelope. The boys roared, and Weir strode off in high dudgeon.

That day Duncan purchased a box of pink en-velopes, and, being expert with a pen, he imitated the neat handwriting and addressed pink enve-lopes to every boy in the training house. Next morning no one except Weir seemed in a hurry to answer the postman's ring. He came in with the letters and his jaw dropping. It so happened that his letter was the very last one, and when he got to it the truth flashed over him. Then the peculiar appropriateness of the nickname Puff was plainly manifest. One by one the boys slid off their chairs to the floor, and at last Weir had to join in the laugh on him.

Each of the boys in turn became the victim of some prank. Raymond betrayed Ken's abhorrence of any kind of perfume, and straightway there was a stealthy colloquy. Cheap perfume of a most pen-etrating and paralyzing odor was liberally pur-chased. In Ken's absence from his room all the clothing that he did not have on his back was saturated. Then the conspirators waited for him to come up the stoop, and from their hiding place in a window of the second floor they dropped an extra quart upon him.

Ken vowed vengeance that would satisfy him thrice over, and he bided his time until he learned who had perpetrated the outrage.

One day after practice his opportunity came. Raymond, Weir, and Trace, the guilty ones, went with Ken to the training quarters to take the steam bath that Murray insisted upon at least once every week. It so turned out that the four were the only players there that afternoon. While the others were undressing, Ken bribed Scotty to go out on an errand, and he let Murray into his scheme. Now, Murray not only had acquired a strong liking for Ken, but he was exceedingly fond of a joke.

"All I want to know," whispered Ken, "is if I might stew them too much—really scald them, you know?"

"No danger," whispered Murray. "That'll be the fun of it. You can't hurt them. But they'll think they're dying."

He hustled Raymond, Weir, and Trace into the tanks and fastened the lids, and carefully tucked towels round their necks to keep in the steam.

"Lots of stew today," he said, turning the handles. "Hello! Where's Scotty? . . . Peg, will you watch these boys a minute while I step out?"

"You bet I will," called Ken to the already disappearing Murray.

The three cooped-in boys looked askance at Ken.

"Wull, I'm not much stuck—" Raymond began glibly enough, and then, becoming conscious that he might betray an opportunity to Ken, he swallowed his tongue.

"What'd you say?" asked Ken, pretending curiosity. Suddenly he began to jump up and down. "Oh, my! Hullabelee! Schoodoorady! What a chance! You gave it away!"

"Look what he's doing!" yelled Trace.

"Hyar!" added Weir.

"Keep away from those pipes!" chimed in Raymond.

"Boys, I've been laying for you, but I never thought I'd get a chance like this. If Murray only stays out three minutes—just three minutes!"

"Three minutes! You idiot, you won't keep us in here that long?" asked Weir in alarm.

"Oh no, not at all. . . . Puff, I think you can stand a little more steam."

Ken turned the handle on full.

"Kel, a first-rate stewing will be good for your daily grouch."

To the accompaniment of Raymond's threats he turned the second handle.

"Trace, you little poll-parrot, you will throw perfume on me? Now roast!"

The heads of the imprisoned boys began to jerk and bob around, and their faces began to take on a flush. Ken leisurely surveyed them and then did an Indian war dance in the middle of the room.

"Here, let me out! Ken, you know how delicate I am," implored Raymond.

"I couldn't entertain the idea for a second," replied Ken.

"I'll lick you!" yelled Raymond.

"My lad, you've got a brainstorm," returned Ken in grieved tones. "Not in the wildest flights of your nightmares have you ever said anything so impossible as that."

"Ken, dear Ken, dear old Peggie," cried Trace, "you know I've got a skinned place on my hip where I slid yesterday. Steam isn't good for that, Worry says. He'll be sore. You must let me out."

"I intend to see, Willie, that you'll be sore too, and skinned all over," replied Ken.

"Open this lid! At once!" roared Weir in sudden anger. His big eyes rolled.

"Bah!" taunted Ken.

Then all three began to roar at Ken at once. "Brute! Devil! Help! Help! Help! We'll fix you for this! . . . It's hotter! it's fire! Aghh! Ouch! Oh! Ah-h-h! . . . O-o-o-o! . . . MURDER! MURDER-R!"

At this juncture Murray ran in.

"What on earth! Peg, what did you do?"

"I only turned on the steam full tilt," replied Ken, innocently.

"Why, you shouldn't have done that," said Murray in pained astonishment.

"Stop talking about it! Let me out!" shrieked Raymond.

Ken discreetly put on his coat and ran from the room.

· 14 ·

THE HERNE GAME

ON the morning of the first of June, the day scheduled for the opening game with Herne, Worry Arthurs had Ken Ward closeted with Homans and Reddy Ray. Worry was trying his best to be soberly calculating in regard to the outcome of the game. He was always trying to impress Ken with the uncertainty of baseball. But a much younger and less observing boy than Ken could have seen through the coach. Worry was dead sure of the result, certain that the day would see a great gathering of Wayne students, and he could not hide his happiness. And the more he betrayed himself the more he growled at Ken.

"Well, we ain't goin' to have that balloon ascension today, are we?" he demanded. "Here we've got down to the big games, and you haven't been up in the air yet. I tell you it ain't right."

"But, Worry, I couldn't go off my head and get rattled just to please you, could I?" implored Ken. To Ken this strain of the coach's had grown to be as serious as it was funny.

"Aw! talk sense," said Worry. "Why, you haven't pitched to a college crowd yet. Wait! Wait till you see that crowd over at Place next week! Thousands of students crazier 'n Indians, and a flock of girls that'll make you bite your tongue off. Ten thousand yellin' all at once."

"Let them yell," replied Ken; "I'm aching to pitch before a crowd. It has been pretty lonesome at Grant Field all season."

"Let 'em yell, eh?" retorted Worry. "All right, my boy, it's comin' to you. And if you lose your head and get slammed all over the lot, don't come to me for sympathy."

"I wouldn't. I can take a licking. Why, Worry, you talk as if—as if I'd done something terrible. What's the matter with me? I've done every single thing you wanted—just as well as I could do it. What are you afraid of?"

"You're gettin' swelled on yourself," said the coach deliberately.

The blood rushed to Ken's face until it was scarlet. He was so astounded and hurt that he could not speak. Worry looked at him once, then, turning hastily away, he walked to the window.

"Peg, it ain't much wonder," he went on smoothly, "and I'm not holdin' it against you. But I want you to forget yourself—"

"I've never had a thought of myself," retorted Ken hotly.

"I want you to go in today like—like an auto-

156

matic machine," went on Worry, as if Ken had not spoken. "There'll be a crowd out, the first of the season. Mebbe they'll throw a fit. Anyway, it's our first big game. As far as the university goes, this is our trial. The students are up in the air; they don't know what to think. Mebbe there won't be a cheer at first. . . . But, Peg, if we beat Herne today they'll tear down the bleachers."

"Well, all I've got to say is that you can order new lumber for the bleachers—because we're going to win," replied Ken, with a smouldering fire in his eyes.

"There you go again! If you're not stuck on yourself, it's too much confidence. You won't be so chipper about three this afternoon, mebbe. Listen! The Herne players got into town last night, and some of them talked a little. It's just as well you didn't see the morning papers. It came to me straight that Gallagher, the captain, and Stern, the first baseman, said you were pretty good for a kid freshman, but a little too swelled to stand the gaff in a big game. They expect you to explode before the third innin'. I wasn't goin' to tell you, Peg, but you're so—"

"They said that, did they?" cried Ken. He jumped up with paling cheek and blazing eye, and the big hand he shoved under Worry's nose trembled like a shaking leaf. "What I won't do to them will be funny! Swelled! Explode! Stand the gaff! Look here, Worry, maybe it's true, but I don't believe it. . . . *I'll beat this Herne team!* Do you get that?"

"Now you're talkin'," replied Worry, with an entire change of manner. "You saw the Herne bunch play. They can field, but how about hittin'?"

"Gallagher, Stern, Hill, and Burr are the veterans of last year's varsity," went on Ken rapidly, as one who knew his subject. "They can hit—if they get what they like."

"Now you're talkin'. How about Gallagher?"

"He hits speed. He couldn't hit a slowball with a paddle."

"Now you're talkin'. There's Stern, how'd you size him?"

"He's weak on a low curve, in or out, or a drop."

"Peg, you're talkin' some now. How about Hill?"

"Hill is a bunter. A high ball in close, speedy, would tie him in a knot."

"Come on, hurry! There's Burr."

"Burr's the best of the lot, a good waiter and hard hitter, but he invariably hits a high curve up in the air."

"All right. So far so good. How about the rest of the team?"

"I'll hand them up a straight, easy ball and let them hit. I tell you I've got Herne beaten, and if Gallagher or anyone else begins to rag me I'll laugh in his face."

"Oh, you will? . . . Say, you go down to your room now, and stay there till time for lunch. Study or read. Don't think another minute about this game."

Ken strode soberly out of the room.

It was well for Ken that he did not see what happened immediately after his exit. Worry and Homans fell into each other's arms.

"Say, fellows, how I hated to do it!" Worry choked with laughter and contrition. "It was the hardest task I ever had. But, Cap, you know we had to make Peg sore. He's too blamed good-natured. Oh, but didn't he take fire! He'll make some of those Herne guys play low-bridge today. Wouldn't it be great if he gave Gallagher the laugh?"

"Worry, don't you worry about that," said Homans. "And it would please me, too, for Gallagher is about as wordy and pompous as any captain I've seen."

"I think you were a little hard on Ken," put in Reddy. His quiet voice drew Worry and Homans from their elation. "Of course, it was necessary to rouse Ken's fighting blood, but you didn't choose the right way. You hurt his feelings. You know, Worry, that the boy is not in the least swelled."

" 'Course I know it, Reddy. Why, Peg's too modest. But I want him to be dead in earnest today. Mind you, I'm thinkin' of Place. He'll beat

159

Herne to a standstill. I worked on his feelin's just to get him all stirred up. You know there's always the chance of rattles in any young player, especially a pitcher. If he's mad he won't be so likely to get 'em. So I hurt his feelin's. I'll make it up to him, don't you fear for that, Reddy."

"I wish you had waited till we go over to Place next week," replied Ray. "You can't treat him that way twice. Over there's where I would look for his weakening. But it may be he won't ever weaken. If he ever does it'll be because of the crowd and not the players."

"I think so, too. A yellin' mob will be new to Peg. But, fellows, I'm only askin' one game from Herne and one, or a good close game, from Place. That'll give Wayne the best record ever made. Look at our standin' now. Why, the newspapers are havin' a fit. Since I picked the varsity we haven't lost a game. Think of that! Those early games don't count. We've had an unbroken string of victories, Peg pitchin' twelve, and Schoonover four. And if wet grounds and other things hadn't canceled other games we'd have won more."

"Yes, we're in the stretch now, Worry, and running strong. We'll win three out of these four big games," rejoined Reddy.

"Oh, say, that'd be too much! I couldn't stand it! Oh, say, Cap, don't you think Reddy, for once, is talkin' about as swift as he sprints?"

"I'm afraid to tell you, Worry," replied Homans

earnestly. "When I look back at our work I can't realize it. But it's time to wake up. The students over at the college are waking up. They will be out today. You are the one to judge whether we're a great team or not. We keep on making runs. It's runs that count. I think, honestly, Worry, that after today we'll be in the lead for championship honors. And I hold my breath when I tell you."

It was remarkably quiet about the training house all that morning. The coach sent a light lunch to the boys in their rooms. They had orders to be dressed, and to report in the reading room at one-thirty.

Raymond came down promptly on time.

"Where's Peg?" asked Worry.

"Why, I thought he was here, ahead of me," replied Raymond in surprise.

A quick survey of the uniformed players proved the absence of Ken Ward and Reddy Ray. Worry appeared startled out of speech, and looked help-lessly at Homans. Then Ray came downstairs, bat in one hand, shoes and glove in the other. He seated himself upon the last step and leisurely proceeded to put on his shoes.

"Reddy, did you see Peg?" asked Worry anxiously.

"Sure, I saw him," replied the sprinter.

"Well?" growled the coach. "Where is he? Sulkin' because I called him?"

"Not so you'd notice it," answered Reddy, in

his slow, careless manner. "I just woke him up."

"What!" yelled Arthurs.

"Peg came to my room after lunch and went to sleep. I woke him just now. He'll be down in a minute."

Worry evidently could not reply at the moment, but he began to beam.

"What would Gallagher say to that?" asked Captain Homans with a smile. "Wayne's varsity pitcher asleep before a Herne game! Oh no, I guess that's not pretty good! Worry, could you ask any more?"

"Cap, I'll never open my face to him again," blurted out the coach.

Ken appeared at the head of the stairs and had started down when the doorbell rang. Worry opened the door to admit Murray, the trainer; Dale, the old varsity captain; and the magnificently built Stevens, guard and captain of the football team.

"Hello, Worry!" called out Murray cheerily. "How're the kids? Boys, you look good to me. Trim and fit, and all cool and quiet-like. Reddy, be careful of your ankles and legs today. After the meet next week you can cut loose and run bases like a blue streak."

Dale stepped forward, earnest and somewhat concerned, but with a winning frankness.

"Worry, will you let Stevens and me sit on the bench with the boys today?"

Worry's face took on the color of a thunder-cloud. "I'm not the captain," he replied. "Ask Homans."

"How about it, Roy?" queried Dale.

Homans was visibly affected by surprise, pleasure, and something more. While he hesitated, perhaps not trusting himself to reply quickly, Stevens took a giant stride to the fore.

"Homans, we've got a hunch that Wayne's going to win," he said, in a deep bass voice. "A few of us have been tipped off, and we got it straight. But the students don't know it yet. So Dale and I thought we'd like them to see how we feel about it—before this game. You've had a rotten deal from the students this year. But they'll more than make it up when you beat Herne. The whole college is waiting and restless."

Homans, recovering himself, faced the two captains courteously and gratefully, and with a certain cool dignity.

"Thank you, fellows! It's fine of you to offer to sit with us on the bench. I thank you on behalf of the varsity. But—not today. All season we've worked and fought without support, and now we're going to beat Herne without support. When we've done that, you and Dale—all the college— can't come too quick to suit us."

"I think I'd say the same thing, if I were in your place," said Dale. "And I'll tell you right here that when I was captain I never plugged any harder to win than I'll plug today."

Then these two famous captains of championship teams turned to Homans' players and eyed them keenly, their faces working, hands clenched, their powerful frames vibrating with the feeling of the moment. That moment was silent, eloquent. It linked Homans' team to the great athletic fame of the university. It radiated the spirit to conquer, the glory of past victories, the strength of honorable defeats. Then Dale and Stevens went out, leaving behind them a charged atmosphere.

"I ain't got a word to say," announced Worry to the players.

"And I've very little," added Captain Homans. "We're all on edge, and being drawn down so fine we may be overeager. Force that back. It doesn't matter if we make misplays. We've made many this season, but we've won all the same. At the bat, remember to keep a sharp eye on the baserunner, and when he signals he is going down, bunt or hit to advance him. That's all."

Ken Ward walked to the field between Worry Arthurs and Reddy Ray. Worry had no word to say, but he kept a tight grip on Ken's arm.

"Peg, I've won many a sprint by not underestimating my opponent," said Reddy quietly. "Now you go at Herne for all you're worth from the start."

When they entered the field there were more spectators in the stands than had attended all the other games together. In a far corner the Herne players in dark blue uniforms were practicing batting. Upon the moment the gong called them in for their turn at field practice. The Wayne team batted and bunted a few balls, and then Homans led them to the bench.

Upon near view the grandstand and bleachers seemed a strange sight to Ken Ward. He took one long look at the black-and-white mass of students behind the backstop, at the straggling lines leading to the gates, at the rapidly filling rows to right and left, and then he looked no more. Already an immense crowd was present. Still it was not a typical college baseball audience. Ken realized that at once. It was quiet, orderly, expectant, and watchful. Very few girls were there. The students as a body had warmed to curiosity and interest, but not to the extent of bringing the girls. After that one glance Ken resolutely kept his eyes upon the ground. He was conscious of a feeling that he wanted to spring up and leap at something. And he brought all his will to force back his overeagerness. He heard the crack of the ball, the shouts of the Herne players, the hum of voices in the grandstand, and the occasional cheers of Herne rooters. There were no Wayne cheers.

"Warm up a little," said Worry in his ear.

Ken peeled off his sweater and walked out with

Dean. A long murmur ran throughout the stands. Ken heard many things said of him, curiously, wonderingly, doubtfully, and he tried not to hear more. Then he commenced to pitch to Dean. Worry stood near him and kept whispering to hold in his speed and just to use his arm easily. It was difficult, for Ken felt that his arm wanted to be cracked like a buggy whip.

"That'll do," whispered Worry. "We're only takin' five minutes' practice. . . . Say, but there's a crowd! Are you all right, Peg—cool-like and determined? . . . Good! Say—but Peg, you'd better look these fellows over."

"I remember them all," replied Ken. "That's Gallagher on the end of the bench; Burr is third from him; Stern's fussing over the bats, and there's Hill, the light-headed fellow, looking this way. There's—"

"That'll do," said Worry. "There goes the gong. It's all off now. Homans has chosen to take the field. I guess mebbe you won't show 'em how to pitch a new white ball! Get at 'em now!" Then he called Ken back as if impelled and whispered to him in a husky voice: "It's been tough for you and for me. Listen! Here's where it begins to be sweet."

Ken trotted out to the box, to the encouraging voices of the infield, and he even caught Reddy Ray's low, rousing call from the far outfield.

"Play!" With the ringing order, which quieted

the audience, the umpire tossed a white ball to Ken.

For a single instant Ken trembled ever so slightly in all his limbs, and the stands seemed a revolving black-and-white band. Then the emotion was as if it had never been. He stepped upon the slab, keen-sighted, cool, and with his pitching game outlined in his mind.

Burr, the curly-haired leader of Herne's batting list, took his position to the left of the plate. Ken threw him an underhand curve, sweeping high and over the inside corner. Burr hit a lofty fly to Homans. Hill, the bunter, was next. For him Ken shot one straight over the plate. Hill let it go by, and it was a strike. Ken put another in the same place, and Hill, attempting to bunt, fouled a little fly, which Dean caught. Gallagher strode third to bat. He used a heavy club, stood right-handed over the plate, and looked aggressive. Ken gave the captain a long study and then swung slowly, sending up a ball that floated like a feather. Gallagher missed it. On the second pitch he swung heavily at a slow curve far off the outside. For a third Ken tried the speedy drop, and the captain, letting it go, was out on strikes.

The sides changed. Worry threw a sweater around Ken.

"The ice's broke, Peg, and you've got your control. That settles it."

Homans went up, to a wavering ripple of applause. He drew two balls and then a strike from Murphy, and hit the next hard toward short. Frick fumbled the ball, recovered it, and threw beautifully, but too late to catch Homans. Raymond sacrificed, sending his captain to second. Murphy could not locate the plate for Reddy Ray and let him get to first on four balls. Weir came next. Homans signed he was going to run on the first pitch. Weir, hitting with the runner, sent a double into right field, and Homans and Ray scored. The bleachers cheered. Homans ran down to third base to the coaching lines, and Ray went to first base. Both began to coach the runner. Dean hit into short field, and was thrown out, while Weir reached third on the play.

"Two out, now! Hit!" yelled Homans to Blake.

Blake hit safely over second, scoring Weir. Then Trace flied out to left field.

"Three runs!" called Homans. "Boys, that's a start! Three more runs and this game's ours! Now, Peg, now!"

Ken did not need that encouragement *now*. The look in Worry's eyes had been enough. He threw speed to Halloway, and on the third ball retired him, Raymond to McCord. Stern came second to bat. In Ken's mind this player was recorded with a weakness on low curves. And Ken found it with two balls pitched. Stern popped up to Blake. Frick, a new player to Ken, let a strike go by, and missed a drop curve and a fastball.

"They can't touch you, Ken," called Raymond, as he tossed aside his glove.

Faint cheers rose from scattered parts of the grandstand, and here and there shouts and yells. The audience appeared to stir, to become animated, and the Herne players settled down to more sober action on the field.

McCord made a bid for a hit, but failed because of fast work by Stern. Ken went up, eager to get to first in any way. He let Murphy pitch, and at last, after fouling several good ones, he earned his base on balls. Once there, he gave Homans the sign that he would run on the first pitch, and he got a fair start. He heard the crack of the ball and saw it glinting between short and third. Running hard, he beat the throw-in to third. With two runners on base, Raymond hit to deep short. Ken went out trying to reach home. Again Reddy Ray came up and got a base on balls, filling the bases. The crowd began to show excitement, and seemed to be stifling cheers in suspense. Weir hurried to bat, his shock of hair waving at every step. He swung hard on the first ball, and, missing it, whirled down, bothering the catcher. Homans raced home on a half passed ball. Then Weir went out on a fly to center.

"Peg, keep at them!" called Reddy Ray. "We've got Murphy's measure."

It cost Ken an effort to deliberate in the box, to think before he pitched. He had to fight his eagerness. But he wasted few balls, and struck Mercer out. Van Sant hit to Weir, who threw wild to first, allowing the runner to reach third. Murphy, batting next, hit one which Ken put straight over the plate, and it went safe through second, scoring Van Sant. The Herne rooters broke out in loud acclaim. Burr came up, choking his bat up short. Again Ken gave him the high, wide curve. He let it pass and the umpire called it a strike. Ken threw another, a little outside this time. Evidently Burr was trying out Ken's control.

"He can't put them over!" yelled Gallagher, from the coaching line. "Here's where he goes up! Wait him out, Burr. Good eye, old man! Here's where we explode the freshman!"

Ken glanced at Gallagher and laughed. Then he sped up another high curve, which the umpire called a strike.

"That's the place, Peg! Put another there!" floated from Reddy in the outfield.

Burr swung viciously, hitting a bounder toward second base. Raymond darted over, went down with his birdlike quickness, came up with the ball, and then he touched the bag and threw to first. It was a play in which he excelled. The umpire called both runners out, retiring the side. A short, sharp yell, like a bark, burst from the bleachers.

Worry was smilingly thoughtful as his boys trotted in to bat.

"Say, if you get a couple of runs this time we'll be *It*. Look at the students. Ready to fall out of the stands. . . . Peg, I'm glad Herne got a run. Now we won't think of a shutout. That'll steady us up. And, boys, break loose now, for the game's ours."

Dean started off with a clean single. On the first pitch he broke for second, and had to slide to make it, as Blake missed the strike. Then Blake went out to first. Trace walked. McCord poked a little fly over the infield, scoring Dean. Ken fouled out. The unerring Homans again hit safely, sending Trace in. With two out and McCord on third and Homans on second, Raymond laid down a beautiful bunt, tallying McCord. And when the Herne catcher tried to head Homans from making third Raymond kept on toward second. It was a daring dash, and he dove to the bag with a long slide, but the decision was against him.

The coach called Homans, Ward, and Ray to him and gathered them close together.

"Boys, listen!" he said, low and tense. "MacNeff and Prince, of Place, are in the grandstand just behind the plate. They're up there to get a line on Peg. We'll fool 'em, and make 'em sick in the bargain. Peg, you let out this innin' and show up the first three hitters. Then I'll take you out and let Schoonover finish the game. See?"

"Take me—out?" echoed Ken.

"That's it, if you make these next three hitters

171

look like monkeys. Don't you see? We've got the Herne game cinched. We don't need to use our star twirler. See? That'll be a bone for Place to chew on. How about it, Cap? What do you think, Reddy?"

"Oh, Worry, if we dared to do it!" Homans exclaimed under his breath. "Herne would never get over it. And it would scare Place to death. . . . But, Worry, Reddy, dare we risk it?"

"It's playin' into our very hands," replied Worry. His hazel eyes were afire with inspiration.

Reddy Ray's lean jaw bulged.

"Homans, it's the trick, and we can turn it."

"What's the score—7 to 1?" muttered Homans. It was a tight place for him, and he seemed tortured between ambition and doubt.

"That fellow Murphy hasn't got one in my groove yet," said Reddy. "I'm due to lace one. We're good for more runs."

That decided Homans. He patted Ken on the shoulder and led him out to the box, but he never spoke a word.

Ken felt like a wild colt just let loose. He faced Hill with a smile, and then, taking his long, overhand swing, he delivered the jump ball. Hill made no move. The umpire called strike. The crowd roared. Ken duplicated the feat. Then Hill missed the third strike. Gallagher walked up doggedly, and Ken smiled at him, too. Then using three wicked, darting drops, Ken struck Gallagher out.

"That's twice!" called Reddy's penetrating voice from the outfield. "Give him a paddle!"

Halloway drew two balls and then three strikes.

Ken ran for the bench amid an uproar most strange and startling to his untried ear. The long, tardy, and stubborn students had broken their silence.

Dale leaped out of the grandstand to lead the cheering. The giant Stevens came piling out of the bleachers to perform a like office. And then they were followed by Bryan, captain of the crew, and Hilbrandt, captain of the track team. Four captains of Wayne teams inspiriting and directing the cheering! Ken's bewildered ears drank in one long, thundering *"Ward! Ward! Ward!"* and then his hearing seemed drowned. The whole mass of students and spectators rose as one, and the deafening stamp of feet only equaled the roar of voices. But now the volume of sound was regular and rhythmic. It was like the approach of a terrible army. For minutes, while the umpire held play suspended, the Wayne supporters in hoarse and stamping tumult came into their own again. It was a wild burst of applause, and as it had been long delayed, so now it was prolonged fiercely to the limit of endurance.

When those waves of sound had rolled away Ken Ward felt a difference in Grant Field, in the varsity, in himself. A different color shone from the sky.

Ken saw Reddy Ray go to bat and drive the ball against the right-field fence. Then as the sprinter got into his wonderful stride once more the whole audience rose in yelling, crashing clamor. And when on Weir's fly to the outfield Reddy raced in to the plate, making the throw-in look feeble, again the din was terrific.

As one in a glorious dream, Ken Ward crouched upon the bench and watched the remainder of that game. He grasped it all as if baseball was all that made life worth living, and as if every moment was his last. He never thought of himself. He was only a part of the team, and that team, every moment, grew sharper, faster, fiercer. He reveled in the game. Schoonover was hit hard, but fast play by Raymond and Weir kept Herne's score down. The little second baseman was here, there, everywhere, like a glint of light. Herne made runs, but Wayne also kept adding runs. Blake caught a foul fly off the bleachers; Trace made a beautiful catch; McCord was like a tower at first base, and little Dean went through the last stages of development that made him a star.

Once in the eighth inning Ken became aware that Worry was punching him in the back and muttering:

"Look out, Peg! Listen! Murphy'll get one in Reddy's groove this time. . . . Oh-h!"

The crack of the ball, as well as Worry's yell, told Ken what had happened. Besides, he could see, and as the ball lined away for the fence, and the sprinter leaped into action, Ken jumped up and screamed:

"Oh, Reddy, it's over—over! No! Run! Run! Oh-h-h!"

In the shrill, piercing strife of sound Ken's scream seemed only a breath at his ears. He held to it, almost splitting his throat, while the sprinter twinkled around third base and came home like a thunderbolt.

Another inning passed, a confusion of hits, throws, runs, and plays to Ken, and then Worry was pounding him again.

"Dig for the trainin' house!" yelled Worry, mouth on his ear. "The students are crazy! They'll eat us alive! They're tearin' the bleachers down! Run for it, Peg!"

· 15 ·

A MATTER OF PRINCIPLE

KEN found himself running across Grant Field, pursued by a happy, roaring mob of students. They might have been Indians, judging from the way Ken and his fellow players fled before them. The trained athletes distanced their well-meaning but violent pursuers and gained the gate, but it was a close shave. The boys bounded up the street into the training house and locked the door till the puffing Arthurs arrived. They let him in and locked the door again.

In another moment the street resounded with the rush of many feet and the yells of frantic students. Murray, the trainer, forced a way through the crowd and up the stoop. He closed and barred the outside door, and then pounded upon the inside door for admittance. Worry let him in.

"They'd make a bowl fight or a football rush look tame," panted Murray. "Hey! Scotty—lock up tight down in the basement. For Heaven's sake don't let that push get in on us! Lock the windows in the front."

"Who's that poundin' on the door?" yelled Worry. He had to yell, for the swelling racket outside made ordinary conversation impossible.

"Don't open it!" shouted Murray. "What do we care for team captains, college professors, athletic directors, or students? They're all out there, and they're crazy, I tell you. I never saw the like. It'd be more than I want to get in that jam. And it'd never do for the varsity. Somebody would get crippled for sure. I'm training this baseball team."

Murray, in his zealous care for his athletes, was somewhat overshooting the mark, for not one of the boys had the slightest desire to be trusted to the mob outside. In fact, Ken looked dazed, and Raymond was scared to the point of trembling; Trace was pale; and all the others, except Homans and Reddy Ray, showed perturbation. Nor were the captain and sprinter deaf to the purport of that hour; only in their faces shone a kindling glow and flush.

By and by the boys slipped to their rooms, removed their uniforms, dressed and crept downstairs like burglars and went in to dinner. Outside the uproar, instead of abating, gathered strength as time went by. At the dinner table the boys had to yell in each other's ears. They had to force what they ate. No one was hungry. When Worry rose from the table they all flocked after him.

It was growing dark outside, and a red glow,

brightening upon the windows, showed the students had lighted bonfires.

"They're goin' to make a night of it," yelled Worry.

"How'll my boys be able to sleep?" shouted Murray. Both coach and trainer were as excited as any of the boys.

"The street's packed solid. Listen!"

The tramp, tramp, tramp of thousands of feet keeping time was like the heavy tread of a marching multitude. Then the tramp died away in a piercing cheer, *"Wayne!"* nine times, clear and sustained—a long, beautiful college cheer. In the breathing spell that followed, the steady tramp of feet went on. One by one, at intervals, the university yells were given, the broken rattling rally, the floating melodious crew cheer, and the hoarse, smashing boom of football. Then again the spirited *"Wayne!"* nine times. After that came shrill calls for the varsity, for Homans, Reddy Ray, Raymond, and Peggie Ward.

"Come upstairs to the windows, boys!" shouted Worry. "We've got to show ourselves."

Worry threw up the windows in Weir's room, and the boys gingerly poked their heads out. A roar greeted their appearance. The heads all popped in as if they had been struck.

"Homans, you'll have to make a speech," cried the coach.

"I will not!"

"You've got to say somethin'. We can't have this crazy gang out here all night."

Then Worry and Murray coaxed and led Homans to the window. The captain leaned out and said something that was unintelligible in the hubbub without. The crowd cheered him and called for Reddy, Ward, and Raymond. Worry grasped the second baseman and shoved him half over the sill. Raymond would have fallen out but for the coach's strong hold.

"Come on, Peg!" yelled Worry.

"Not on your life!" cried Ken, in fright. He ran away from the coach and dived under the bed. But Reddy Ray dragged him out and to the window, and held him up in the bright bonfire glare. Then he lifted a hand to silence the roaring crowd.

"Fellows, here he is—Worry's demon, Wayne's pitcher!" called Reddy, in ringing, far-reaching voice. "Listen! Peggie didn't lose his nerve when he faced Herne today, but he's lost it now. He's lost his voice, too. But he says for you to go away and save your cheers for this day in two weeks, when we meet Place. Then, he says, you'll have something to cheer for!"

The crafty sprinter knew how to appeal to the students. All the voice and strength and enthusiasm left in them went up in a mighty bawl that rattled the windows and shook the house. They finished with nine "*Wayne!*"s and a long, rousing "*Peggie Ward!*" and then they went away.

"By George! look here, Peg," said Reddy, earnestly, "they gave you Wayne's Nine! *Wayne's Nine!* Do you hear? I never knew a freshman varsity man to get that cheer."

"You've got to beat Place now, after tellin' 'em you'd do it," added Worry.

"But, Worry, I didn't say a word—it was Reddy," replied Ken in distress.

"Same thing," rejoined the coach. "Now, boys, let's quiet down and talk over the game. I won't waste any time jollyin' you. I couldn't praise you enough if I spent the rest of the season tryin' to. One and all, by yourselves and in a bunch, you played Herne off their feet. I'll bet MacNeff and Prince are dizzy figurin' what'll happen Saturday week. As to the score, why, scores don't mean much to us—"

"What was the score, anyway?" asked Ken.

The boys greeted this with shouts of doubtful laughter, and Worry glanced with disapproval at his star.

"Peg, you keep me guessin' a lot. But not to know how much we beat Herne would be more'n I could stand. On the level, now, don't you know the score?"

"Fair and square, I don't, Worry. You never would let me think of how many runs we had or needed. I can count seven—yes, and one more, that was Reddy's home run."

"Peg, you must have been up in the air a little;

14 to 4, that's it. And we didn't take our bat in the last of the ninth."

Then followed Worry's critical account of the game, and a discussion in which the boys went over certain plays. During the evening many visitors called, but did not gain admission. The next morning, however, Worry himself brought in the newspapers, which heretofore he had forbidden the players to read, and he told them they were now free to have any callers or to go where they liked. There was a merry scramble for the papers, and presently the reading room was as quiet as a church.

The account that held Ken Ward in rapt perusal was the *Morning Times-Star*'s. At first the print blurred in Ken's sight. Then he read it over again. He liked the glowing praise given the team and was shamefully conscious of the delight in his name in large letters. A third time he read it, guiltily this time, for he did not dream that his comrades were engrossed in like indulgence.

WAYNE OUTCLASSES HERNE

ARTHURS DEVELOPS ANOTHER GREAT TEAM. PEGGIE WARD AND REDDY RAY STARS

Wayne defeated Herne yesterday 14 to 4, and thereby leaped into the limelight. It was a surprise to everyone, Herne most of all. Owing to the stringent eligibility rules now in force at

Wayne, and the barring of the old varsity, nothing was expected of this season's team. Arthurs, the famous coach, has built a wonderful nine out of green material, and again establishes the advisability of professional coaches for the big universities.

With one or two exceptions Wayne's varsity is made up of players developed this year. Homans, the captain, was well known about town as an amateur player of ability. But Arthurs has made him into a great field captain and a base-getter of remarkable skill. An unofficial computing gives him the batting average of .536. No captain or any other player of any big college team in the East ever approached such percentage as that. It is so high that it must be a mistake.

Reddy Ray, the intercollegiate champion in the sprints, is the other seasoned player of the varsity, and it is safe to say that he is the star of all the college teams. A wonderful fielder, a sure and heavy hitter, and like a flash on the bases, he alone makes Homans's team formidable.

Then there is Peg Ward, Worry Arthurs's demon pitcher, of freshman bowl fight fame. This lad has been arriving since spring, and now he has arrived. He is powerful and has a great arm. He seems to pitch without effort, has twice the speed of Dale, and is as cool in the box as a veteran. But it is his marvelous control of the ball that puts him in a class by himself. In the fourth inning of yesterday's game he extended himself, probably on orders from Coach Arthurs, and struck out Herne's three best hitters on eleven pitched balls. Then he was taken out and Schoonover put in. This whiteheaded lad is no slouch of a pitcher, by the way. But it must have been a bitter pill for Herne to swallow. The proud Herne varsity have been used to knocking pitchers out of the box, instead of seeing them removed because they were too good. Also, MacNeff and Prince, of Place, who saw the game, must have had food for reflection. They did not get much of a line on young Ward, and what they saw will not give them pleasant dreams. We pick Ward to beat the heavy-hitting Place team.

Other youngsters of Arthurs's nine show up well, particularly Raymond and Weir, who have springs in their feet and arms like whips. Altogether Arthurs's varsity is a strangely assorted, wonderfully chosen group of players. We might liken them to the mechanism of a fine watch, with Ward as the mainspring, and the others with big or little parts to perform, but each dependent upon the other. Wayne's greatest baseball team!

Ken read it all thirstily, wonderingly, and recorded it deep in the deepest well of his memory. It seemed a hundred times as sweet for all the misery and longing and fear and toil which it had cost to gain.

And each succeeding day grew fuller and richer with its meed of reward. All the boys of the varsity were sought by the students, Ken most of all. Everywhere he went he was greeted with a regard that made him still more bashful and ashamed. If he stepped into Carlton Hall, it was to be surrounded by a frankly admiring circle of students. He could not get a moment alone in the library. Professors had a smile for him and often stopped to chat. The proudest moment of his college year was when President Halstead met him in the promenade, and before hundreds of students turned to walk a little way with him. There seemed not to be a single student of the university, or anyone connected with it, who did not recognize him. Bryan took him to watch the crew practice; Stevens played billiards with him at the club; Dale openly sought his society. Then the fraternities began to vie with one another for Ken. In all his life he had not imagined a fellow could be treated so well. It was an open secret that Ken Ward was extremely desired in the best fraternities. He could not have counted his friends. Through it all, by thinking of Worry and the big games coming, he managed to stay on his feet.

One morning, when he was at the height of this enjoyable popularity, he read a baseball note that set him to thinking hard. The newspaper, commenting on the splendid results following Wayne's new athletic rules, interpreted one rule in a way astounding to Ken. It was something to the effect that all players who had been *on* a team which paid any player or any expenses of any player were therefore ineligible. Interpretation of the rules had never been of any serious moment to Ken. He had never played on any but boy teams. But suddenly he remembered that during a visit to the mountains with his mother he had gone to a place called Eagle's Nest, a summer hotel colony. It boasted of a good ball team and had a rival in the Glenwoods, a team from an adjoining resort. Ken had been in the habit of chasing flies for the players in practice. One day Eagle's Nest journeyed over to Glenwood to play, and being short one player they took Ken to fill in. He had scarcely started in the game when the regular player appeared, thus relieving him. The incident had completely slipped Ken's mind until recalled by the newspaper note.

Whereupon Ken began to ponder. He scouted the idea of that innocent little thing endangering his eligibility at Wayne. But the rule, thus made clear, stood out in startlingly black-and-white relief. Eagle's Nest supported a team by subscription among the hotel guests. Ken had ridden ten miles in a bus with the team, and had worn one of the uniforms for some few minutes. Therefore, upon a technicality, perhaps, he had been *on* a summer squad, and had no right to play for Wayne.

Ken went to Homans and told him the circumstance. The captain looked exceedingly grave, then getting more particulars he relaxed.

"You're safe, Peg. You're perfectly innocent. But don't mention it to anyone else, especially Worry. He'd have a fit. What a scare you'd throw into the varsity camp! Forget the few minutes you wore that Eagle's Nest suit."

For the time being this reassured Ken, but after a while his anxiety returned. Homans had said not to mention it, and that bothered Ken. He lay awake half of one night thinking about the thing. It angered him and pricked his conscience and roused him. He wanted to feel absolutely sure of his position, for his own sake first of all. So next morning he cornered Worry and blurted out the secret.

"Peg, what're you givin' me!" he ejaculated.

Ken repeated his story, somewhat more clearly and at greater length. Worry turned as white as a ghost.

"Good gracious, Peg, you haven't told anybody?"

"No one but Homans."

Worry gave a long sigh of relief, and his face regained some of its usual florid color.

"Well, that's all right then. . . . Say, didn't I tell you once that I had a weak heart? Peg, of course you're an amateur, or there never was one. But 'em fathead directors! Why, I wouldn't have 'em find that out for a million dollars. They're idiots enough to make a shinin' example of you right before the Place games. Keep it under your hat, see!"

This last was in the nature of a command, and Ken had always religiously obeyed Worry. He went to his room feeling that the matter had been decided for him. Relief, however, did not long abide with him. He began to be torn between loyalty to Worry and duty to himself. He felt guilt-less, but he was not sure of it, and until he was sure he could not be free in mind. Suddenly he thought of being actually barred from the varsity and was miserable. That he could not bear. Strong temptation now assailed Ken and found him weak. A hundred times he reconciled himself to Worry's command, to Homans's point of view, yet every time something rose within him and rebelled. But despite the rebellion Ken almost gave in. He fought off thought of his new sweet popularity, of the glory of being Wayne's athletic star. He fought to look the thing fairly in the face. To him it loomed up a hundredfold larger than an incident of his baseball career. And so he got strength to do the thing that would ease the voice of con-science. He went straight to the coach.

"Worry, I've got to go to the directors and tell them. I—I'm sorry, but I've got to do it."

He expected a storm of rage from Worry, but never had the coach been so suave, so kindly, so magnetic. He called Homans and Raymond and Weir and others who were in the house at the moment and stated Ken's case. His speech flowed smooth and rapid. The matter under his deft ar-gument lost serious proportions. But it seemed to Ken that Worry did not tell the boys the whole truth, or they would not have laughed at the thing and made him out as oversensitive. And Ken was now growing too discouraged and bewildered to tell them. Moreover, he was getting stubborn. The thing was far from a joke. The cunning of the coach proved that. Worry wound the boys around his little finger.

At this juncture Reddy Ray entered the training house.

More than once Ken had gone to the great sprinter with confidences and troubles, and now he began impulsively, hurriedly, incoherently, to tell the story.

"And Reddy," concluded Ken, "I've got to tell the directors. It's something—hard for me to explain. I couldn't pitch another game with this hanging over me. I must—tell them—and take my medicine."

"Sure. It's a matter of principle," replied Reddy, in his soft, slow voice. His keen eyes left Ken's pale face and met the coach's. "Worry, I'll take Peg up to see the athletic faculty. I know Andrews, the president, and he's the one to hear Peg's story."

Worry groaned and sank into a chair, crushed and beaten. Then he swore, something unusual in him. Then he began to rave at the fatheaded directors. Then he yelled that he would never coach another ball team so long as he lived.

Ken followed Reddy out of the training house and along the street. The fact that the sprinter did not say a word showed Ken he was understood, and he felt immeasurably grateful. They crossed the campus and entered College Hall, to climb the winding stairway. To Ken that was a long, hateful climb. Andrews, and another of the directors whom Ken knew by sight, were in the office. They greeted the visitors with cordial warmth.

"Gentlemen," began Reddy, "Ward thinks he has violated one of the eligibility rules."

There was no beating about the bush with Reddy Ray, no shading of fact, no distortion of the truth. Coolly he stated the case. But, strangely to Ken, the very truth, told by Reddy in this way, somehow lost its terrors. Ken's shoulders seemed unburdened of a terrible weight.

Andrews and his colleague laughed heartily.

"You see—I—I forgot all about it," said Ken.

"Yes, and since he remembered he's been worrying himself sick," resumed Reddy. "Couldn't rest till he'd come over here."

"Ward, it's much to your credit that you should confide something there was never any chance of becoming known," said the president of the athletic faculty. "We appreciate it. You may relieve your mind of misgivings as to your eligibility. Even if we tried I doubt if we could twist a rule to affect your standing. And you may rest assured we wouldn't try in the case of so fine a young fellow and so splendid a pitcher for Wayne."

Then Andrews courteously shook hands with Ken and Reddy and bowed them out. Ken danced halfway down the stairway and slid the rest on the bannister.

"Reddy, wasn't he just fine?" cried Ken, all palpitating with joy.

"Well, Peg, Andrews is a nice old thing if you approach him right," replied Reddy dryly. "You wouldn't believe me, would you, if I said I had my heart in my throat when we went in?"

"No, I wouldn't," replied Ken bluntly.

"I thought not," said Reddy. Then the gravity that had suddenly perplexed Ken cleared from the sprinter's face. "Peg, let's have some fun with Worry and the boys."

"I'm in for anything now."

"We'll go back to the training house with long faces. When we get in you run upstairs as if you couldn't face anyone, but be sure to sneak back to the head of the stairs to see and hear the fun. I'll fix Worry, all right. Now, don't flunk. It's a chance."

Ken could not manage to keep a straight face as they went in, so he hid it and rushed upstairs. He bumped into Raymond, knocking him flat.

"Running to a fire again?" growled Raymond.

"Got a fire medal, haven't you? Always falling over people."

Ken tried to simulate ungovernable rage and impotent distress at once. He waved one fist and tore his hair with the other hand.

"Get out of my way!" roared Ken. "What'll you say when I tell you I'm barred from the varsity!"

"Oh! Ken! No, no—don't say it," faltered Raymond, all sympathy in an instant.

Ken ran into his room, closed the door, and then peeped out. He saw Raymond slowly sag downstairs as if his heart was broken. Then Ken slipped out and crawled down the hall till he could see into the reading room. All the boys were there, with anxious faces, crowded around the coach. Worry was livid. Reddy Ray seemed the only calm person in the room and he had tragedy written all over him.

"Out with it!" shouted Worry. "Don't stand there like a mournful preacher. What did 'em fatheads say?"

Reddy threw up his hands with a significant gesture.

"I knew it!" howled Worry, jumping up and down. "I knew it! Why did you take the kid over there? Why didn't you let me and Homans handle this thing? You redheaded, iron-jawed, cold-blooded windchaser! You've done it now, haven't you? I—oh—"

Worry began to flounder helplessly.

"They said a few more things," went on Reddy. "Peg is barred, Raymond is barred, I am barred. I told them about my baseball career out west. The directors said some pretty plain things about you, Worry, I'm sorry to tell. You're a rotten coach. In fact, you ought to be a coach at an undertaker's. Homans gets the credit for the work of the team. They claim you are too hard on the boys, too exacting, too brutal, in fact. Andrews recited a record of your taking sandwiches from us and aiding and abetting Murray in our slow starvation. The directors will favor your dismissal and urge the appointment of Professor Rhodes, who as coach will at least feed us properly."

Reddy stopped to catch his breath and gain time for more invention. Of all the unhappy mortals on earth Worry Arthurs looked the unhappiest. He believed every word as if it had been gospel. And that part about Professor Rhodes was the last straw.

Ken could stand the deception no longer. He marveled at Reddy's consummate lying and how he could ever stand that look on Worry's face. Bounding downstairs four steps at a jump, Ken burst like a bomb upon the sad-faced group.

"Oh, Worry, it's all a joke!"

THE FIRST PLACE GAME

RAIN prevented the second Herne game, which was to have been played on the Herne grounds. It rained steadily all day Friday and Saturday, to the disappointment of Wayne's varsity. The coach, however, admitted that he was satisfied to see the second contest with Herne go by the board.

"I don't like big games away from home," said Worry. "It's hard on new teams. Besides, we beat Herne to death over here. Mebbe we couldn't do it over there, though I ain't doubtin'. But it's Place we're after, and if we'd had that game at Herne we couldn't have kept Place from gettin' a line on us. So I'm glad it rained."

The two Place games fell during a busy week at Wayne. Wednesday was the beginning of the commencement exercises and only a comparatively few students could make the trip to Place. But the night before the team left, the students, four thousand strong, went to the training house and filled a half-hour with college songs and cheers.

Next morning Dale and Stevens, heading a small band of Wayne athletes and graduates, met the team at the railroad station and boarded the train with them. Worry and Homans welcomed them, and soon every Wayne player had two or more for company. Either by accident or design, Ken could not tell which, Dale and Stevens singled him out for their especial charge. The football captain filled one seat with his huge bulk and faced Ken, and Dale sat with a hand on Ken's shoulder.

"Peg, we're backing you for all we're worth," said Stevens. "But this is your first big game away from home. It's really the toughest game of the season. Place is a hard nut to crack any time. And her players on their own backyard are scrappers who can take a lot of beating and still win out. Then there's another thing that's no small factor in their strength: They are idolized by the students, and rooting at Place is a science. They have a yell that beats anything you ever heard. It'll paralyze a fellow at a critical stage. But that yell is peculiar in that it rises out of circumstances leading to almost certain victory. That is, Place has to make a strong bid for a close, hard game to work up that yell. So if it comes today you be ready for it. Have your ears stuffed with cotton, and don't let that yell blow you up in the air."

Dale was even more earnest than Stevens.

"Peg, Place beat me over here last year, beat me 6–3. They hit me harder than I ever was hit before, I guess. You went down to Washington, Worry said, to look them over. Tell me what you think—how you sized them up."

Dale listened attentively while Ken recited his impressions.

"You've got Prince and MacNeff figured exactly right," replied Dale. "Prince is the football captain, by the way. Be careful how you run into second base. If you ever slide into him headfirst—good-bye! He's a great player, and he can hit any kind of a ball. MacNeff now, just as you said, is weak on a high ball close in, and he kills a low ball. 'Kills' is the word! He hits them a mile. But, Peg, I think you're a little off on Keene, Starke, and Martin, the other Place cracks. They're veterans, hard to pitch to; they make you cut the plate; they are as apt to bunt as hit, and they are fast. They keep a fellow guessing. I think Starke bails out a little on a curve, but the others have no weakness I ever discovered. But, Peg, I expect you to do more with them than I did. My control was never any too good, and you can throw almost as straight as a fellow could shoot a rifle. Then your high fastball, that one you get with the long swing, it would beat any team. Only I'm wondering, I'm asking—can you use it right along, in the face of such coaching and yelling and hitting as you'll run against today? I'm asking deliberately, because I want to give you confidence."

"Why, yes, Dale, I think I can. I'm pretty sure of it. That ball comes easily, only a little longer swing and more snap, and honestly, Dale, I hardly ever think about the plate. I know where it is, and I could shut my eyes and throw strikes."

"Peg, you're a wonder," replied Dale warmly. "If you can do that—and hang me if I doubt it—you will make Place look like a lot of duds. We're sure to make a few runs. Homans and Ray will hit Salisbury hard. There's no fence around Place Field, and every ball Reddy hits past a fielder will be a home run. You can gamble on that. So set a fast clip when you start in, and hang."

Some time later, when Ken had changed seats and was talking to Raymond, he heard Worry say to somebody:

"Well, if Peg don't explode today he never will. I almost wish he would. He'd be better for it afterward."

This surprised Ken, annoyed him, and straightway he became thoughtful. Why this persistent harping on the chance of his getting excited from one cause or another, losing his control and thereby the game? Ken had not felt in the least nervous about the game. He would get so, presently, if his advisers did not stop hinting. Then Worry's wish that he might "explode" was puz-

zling. A little shade of gloom crept over the bright
horizon of Ken's hopes. Almost unconsciously
vague doubts of himself fastened upon him. For
the first time he found himself looking forward to
a baseball game with less eagerness than uncertainty. Stubbornly he fought off the mood.

Place was situated in an old college town famed
for its ancient trees and quaint churches and inns.
The Wayne varsity, arriving late, put on their
uniforms at the St. George, a tavern that seemed
never to have been in any way acquainted with a
college baseball team. It was very quiet and apparently deserted. For that matter the town itself
appeared deserted. The boys dressed hurriedly,
in silence, with frowning brows and compressed
lips. Worry Arthurs remained downstairs while
they dressed. Homans looked the team over and
then said:

"Boys, come on! Today's our hardest game."

It was only a short walk along the shady street
to the outskirts of the town and the athletic field.
The huge stands blocked the view from the back
and side. Homans led the team under the bleachers, through a narrow walled-in aisle, to the side
entrance, and there gave the word for the varsity
to run out upon the field. A hearty roar of applause
greeted their appearance.

Ken saw a beautiful green field, level as a floor,
with a great half-circle of stands and bleachers at
one end. One glance was sufficient to make Ken's

breathing an effort. He saw a glittering mass, a broad, moving band of color. Everywhere waved Place flags, bright gold and blue. White faces gleamed like daisies on a golden slope. In the bleachers close to first base massed a shirtsleeved crowd of students, row on row of them, thousands in number. Ken experienced a little chill as he attached the famous Place yell to that significant placing of rooters. A soft breeze blew across the field, and it carried low laughter and voices of girls, a merry hum and subdued murmur, and an occasional clear shout. The whole field seemed keenly alive.

From the bench Ken turned curious, eager eyes upon the practicing Place men. Never had he regarded players with as sharp an interest, curiosity being mingled with admiration, and confidence with doubt. MacNeff, the captain, at first base, veteran of three years, was a tall, powerful fellow, bold and decisive in action. Prince, Place's star on both gridiron and diamond, played at second base. He was very short, broad and heavy, and looked as if he would have made three of little Raymond. Martin, at shortstop, was of slim, muscular build. Keene and Starke, in center and left, were big men. Salisbury looked all of six feet, and every inch a pitcher. He also played end on the football varsity. Ken had to indulge in a laugh at the contrast in height and weight of Wayne when compared to Place. The laugh was good for him, because it seemed to loosen something hard and tight within his breast. Besides, Worry saw him laugh and looked pleased, and that pleased Ken.

"Husky lot of stiffs, eh, Peg?" said Worry, reading Ken's thought. "But, say! this ain't no football game. We'll make these heavyweights look like ice wagons. I never was much on beefy ballplayers. Aha! there goes the gong. Place's takin' the field. That suits me. . . . Peg, listen! The game's on. I've only one word to say to you. *Try to keep solid on your feet!*"

A short cheer, electrifying in its force, pealed out like a blast.

Then Homans stepped to the plate amid generous handclapping. The Place adherents had their favorites, but they always showed a sportsmanlike appreciation of opponents. Salisbury wound up, took an enormous stride, and pitched the ball. He had speed. Homans seldom hit on the first pitch, and this was a strike. But he rapped the next like a bullet at Griffith, the third baseman. Griffith blocked the ball, and, quickly reaching it, he used a snap underhand throw to first, catching Homans by a narrow margin. It was a fine play and the crowd let out another blast.

Raymond, coming up, began his old trick of trying to work the pitcher for a base. He was small and he crouched down until a wag in the bleachers yelled that this was no kindergarten game. Raymond was exceedingly hard to pitch to. He was always edging over the plate, trying to get hit. If anybody touched him in practice he would roar like a mad bull, but in a game he would cheerfully have stopped cannonballs. He got in front of Salisbury's third pitch, and, dropping his bat, started for first base. The umpire called him back. Thereupon Raymond fouled balls and went through contortions at the plate till he was out on strikes.

When Reddy Ray took his position at bat audible remarks passed like a wave through the audience. Then a long, hearty cheer greeted the great sprinter. When the roar once again subsided into waiting suspense a strong-lunged Wayne rooter yelled, *"Watch him run!"*

The outfielders edged out deeper and deeper. MacNeff called low to Salisbury: "Don't let this fellow walk! Keep them high and make him hit!" It was evident that Place had gotten a line on one Wayne player.

Salisbury delivered the ball and Reddy whirled with his level swing. There was a sharp crack.

Up started the crowd with a sudden explosive: "Oh!"

Straight as a beeline the ball sped to Keene in deep center, and Reddy was out.

Wayne players went running out and Place players came trotting in. Ken, however, at Worry's order, walked slowly and leisurely to the pitcher's box. He received an ovation from the audience that completely surprised him and which stirred him to warm gratefulness. Then, receiving the ball, he drew one quick breath, and faced the stern issue of the day.

As always, he had his pitching plan clearly defined in mind, and no little part of it was cool deliberation, study of the batter to the point of irritating him, and then boldness of action. He had learned that he was not afraid to put the ball over the plate, and the knowledge had made him bold, and boldness increased his effectiveness.

For Keene, the first batter up, Ken pitched his fastball with all his power. Like a glancing streak it shot over. A low whistling ran through the bleachers. For the second pitch Ken took the same long motion, ending in the sudden delivery, but this time he threw a slow, wide, tantalizing curve that floated and waved and circled around across the plate. It also was a strike. Keene had not offered to hit either. In those two balls, perfectly controlled, Ken deliberately showed the Place team the wide extremes of his pitching game.

"Keene, he don't waste any. Hit!" ordered MacNeff from the bench. The next ball, a high curve, Keene hit on the fly to Homans.

The flaxen-haired Prince trotted up with little, short steps. Ken did not need the wild outburst from the crowd to appreciate this sturdy hero of many gridiron and diamond battles. He was so enormously wide, almost as wide as he was long, that he would have been funny to Ken but for the reputation that went with the great shoulders and stumpy legs.

"Ward, give me a good one," said Prince, in a low, pleasant voice. He handled his heavy bat as if it had been light as a yardstick.

It was with more boldness than intention of gratifying Prince that Ken complied, using the same kind of ball he had tried first on Keene. Prince missed it. The next, a low curve, he cracked hard to the left of Raymond. The second baseman darted over, fielded the ball cleanly, and threw Prince out.

Then the long, rangy MacNeff, home run hitter for Place, faced Ken. His position at bat bothered Ken, for he stood almost on the plate. Remembering MacNeff's weakness, Ken lost no time putting a swift toss inside under his chin. The Place captain lunged around at it, grunting with his swing. If he had hit the ball it would have been with the handle of his bat. So Ken, knowing his control, and sure that he could pitch high shoots all day over the inside corner of the plate, had no more fear of the Place slugger. And it took only three more pitches to strike him out.

From that point on the game seesawed inning by inning, Ken outpitching Salisbury, but neither team scored. At intervals cheers marked the good plays of both teams, and time and again the work of the pitchers earned applause. The crowd seemed to be holding back, and while they waited for the unexpected the short, sharp innings slipped by.

Trace for Wayne led off in the seventh with a single over short. Ken, attempting to sacrifice, rolled a little bunt down the third-base line and beat the throw. With no one out and the head of the batting list up, the Wayne players awoke to possibilities. The same fiery intensity that had characterized their play all season now manifested itself. They were all on their feet, and Weir and McCord on the coaching lines were yelling hoarsely at Salisbury, tearing up the grass with their spikes, dashing to and fro, shouting advice to the runners.

"Here's where we score! Oh! you pitcher! We're due to trim you now! Steady, boys, play it safe, play it safe!—don't let them double you!"

Up by the bench Homans was selecting a bat.

"Worry, I'd better dump one," he whispered.

"That's the trick," replied the coach. "Advance them at any cost. There's Reddy to follow."

The reliable Salisbury rolled the ball in his hands, feinted to throw to the bases, and showed his steadiness under fire. He put one square over for Homans and followed it upon the run. Homans made a perfect bunt, but instead of going along either baseline, it went straight into the pitcher's hands. Salisbury whirled and threw to Prince, who covered the bag, and forced Trace. One out and still two runners on bases. The crowd uttered a yell and then quickly quieted down. Raymond bent low over the plate and watched Salisbury's slightest move. He bunted the first ball, and it went foul over the third-base line. He twisted the second toward first base, and it, too, rolled foul. And still he bent low as if to bunt again. The infield slowly edged in closer. But Raymond straightened up on Salisbury's next pitch and lined the ball out. Prince leaped into the air and caught the ball in his gloved hand. Homans dove back into first base; likewise Ken into second, just making it in the nick of time, for Martin was on the run to complete a possible double play. A shout at once hoarse and shrill went up, and heavy clattering thunder rolled along the floor of the bleachers. Two out and still two men on bases.

If there was a calm person on Place Field at that moment it was Reddy Ray, but his eyes glinted like sparks as he glanced at the coach.

"Worry, I'll lace one this time," he said and strode for the plate.

Weir and McCord were shrieking: "Oh, look who's up! Oh-h! Oh-h! Play it safe, boys!"

"Watch him run!"

That came from the same deep-chested individual who had before hinted of the sprinter's fleetness, and this time the Wayne players recognized the voice of Murray. How hopeful and thrilling the suggestion was, coming from him!

The Place infield trotted to deep positions; the outfielders moved out and swung around far to the right. Salisbury settled down in the box and appeared to put on extra effort as he delivered the ball. It was wide. The next also went off the outside of the plate. It looked as if Salisbury meant to pass Reddy to first. Then those on the bench saw a glance and a nod pass between Reddy Ray and Coach Arthurs. Again Salisbury pitched somewhat to the outside of the plate, but this time Reddy stepped forward and swung.

Crack!

Swift as an arrow and close to the ground the ball shot to left field. Starke leaped frantically to head it off, and as it took a wicked bound he dove forward headfirst, hands outstretched, and knocked it down. But the ball rolled a few yards, and Starke had to recover from his magnificent effort.

No one on the field saw Ward and Homans running for the plate. All eyes were on the gray, flitting shadow of a sprinter. One voice only, and that was Murray's, boomed out in the silence. When Reddy turned second base Starke reached the ball and threw for third. It was a beautiful race between ball and runner for the bag. As Reddy stretched into the air in a long slide the ball struck and shot off the ground with a glancing bound. They reached the base at the same time. But Griffith, trying to block the runner, went spinning down, and the ball rolled toward the bleachers. Reddy was up and racing plateward so quickly that it seemed he had not been momentarily checked. The few Wayne rooters went wild.

"Three runs!" yelled the delirious coaches. Weir was so overcome that he did not know it was his turn at bat. When called in he hurried to the plate and drove a line fly to center that Keene caught only after a hard run.

Ken Ward rose from the bench to go out on the diamond. The voices of his comrades sounded far away, as voices in a dream.

"Three to the good now, Ward! It's yours!" said Captain Homans.

"Only nine more batters! Peg, keep your feet leaded!" called Reddy Ray.

"It's the seventh, and Place hasn't made a safe hit! Oh, Ken!" came from Raymond.

So all the boys vented their hope and trust in their pitcher.

There was a mist before Ken's eyes that he could not rub away. The field blurred at times. For five innings after the first he had fought some unaccountable thing. He had kept his speed, his control, his memory of batters, and he had pitched magnificently. But something had hovered over him and had grown more tangible as the game progressed. There was a shadow always before his sight.

In the last of the seventh, with Keene at bat,

Ken faced the plate with a strange unsteadiness and a shrinking for which he hated himself. What was wrong with him? Had he been taken suddenly ill? Anger came to his rescue, and he flung himself into his pitching with fierce ardor. He quivered with a savage hope when Keene swung ineffectually at the high inside pitch. He pitched another and another, and struck out the batter. But now it meant little to see him slam down his bat in a rage. For Ken had a foreboding that he could not do it again. When Prince came up Ken found he was having difficulty in keeping the ball where he wanted it. Prince batted a hot grounder to Blake, who fumbled. MacNeff had three balls and one strike called upon him before he hit hard over second base. But Raymond pounced upon the ball like a tiger, dashed over the bag and threw to first, getting both runners.

"Wull, Ken, make them hit to me," growled Raymond.

Ken sat down upon the bench far from the coach. He shunned Worry in that moment. The warm praise of his fellow players was meaningless to him. Something was terribly wrong. He knew he shrank from going into the box again, yet dared not admit it to himself. He tried to think clearly, and found his mind in a whirl. When the Wayne batters went out in one, two, three order, and it was time for Ken to pitch again, he felt ice form in his veins.

"Only six more hitters!" called Reddy's warning voice. It meant cheer and praise from Reddy, but to Ken it seemed a knell.

"Am I weakening?" muttered Ken. "Am I going up in the air? *What* is wrong with me?"

He was nervous now and could not stand still, and he felt himself trembling. The ball was wet from the sweat in his hands; his hair hung damp over his brow and he continually blew it out of his eyes. With all his spirit he crushed back the almost overwhelming desire to hurry, hurry, hurry. Once more, in a kind of passion, he fought off the dreaded unknown weakness.

With two balls pitched to Starke he realized that he had lost control of his curve. He was not frightened for the loss of his curve, but he went stiff with fear that he might lose control of his fastball, his best and last resort. Grimly he swung and let drive. Starke lined the ball to the left. The crowd lifted itself with a solid roar, and when Homans caught the hit near the foul flag, subsided with a long groan. Ken set his teeth. He knew he was not right, but did anyone else know it? He was getting magnificent support and luck was still with him.

"Over the pan, Peg! Don't waste one!" floated from Reddy warningly.

Then Ken felt sure that Reddy had seen or divined his panic. How soon would the Place players find it out? With his throat swelling and his mouth dry and his whole body in a ferment Ken pitched to Martin. The shortstop hit to Weir, who made a superb stop and throw. Two out!

From all about Ken on the diamond came the low encouraging calls of his comrades. Horton, a burly lefthander, stepped forward, swinging a hefty bat. Ken could no longer steady himself and he pitched hurriedly. One ball, two balls, one strike, three balls—how the big looming Horton stood waiting over the plate! Almost in despair Ken threw again, and Horton smote the ball with a solid rap. It was a low bounder. Raymond pitched forward full length toward first base, and the ball struck in his glove with a crack and stuck there. Raymond got up and tossed it to McCord. A thunder of applause greeted this star play of the game.

The relief was so great that Ken fairly tottered as he went in to the bench. Worry did not look at him. He scarcely heard what the boys said; he felt them patting him on the back. Then to his amazement, and slowly mounting certainty of disaster, the side was out, and it was again his turn to pitch.

"Only three more, Peg! The tail end of the batting list. *Hang on!*" said Reddy, as he trotted out.

Ken's old speed and control momentarily came back to him. Yet he felt he pitched rather by instinct than intent. He struck Griffith out.

"Only two more, Peg!" called Reddy.

The great audience sat in depressed, straining silence. Long since the few Wayne rooters had lost their vocal powers.

Conroy hit a high fly to McCord.

"Oh, Peg, *only one more!*" came the thrilling cry. No other Wayne player could speak a word then.

With Salisbury up, Ken had a momentary flash of his old spirit and he sent a straight ball over the plate, meaning it to be hit. Salisbury did hit it, and safely, through short. The long silent, long waiting crowd opened up with yells and stamping feet.

A horrible, cold, deadly sickness seized upon Ken as he faced the fleet, sure-hitting Keene. He lost his speed, he lost his control. Before he knew what had happened he had given Keene a base on balls. Two on bases and two out!

The Place players began to leap and fling up their arms and scream. When out of their midst Prince ran to the plate a piercing, ear-splitting sound pealed up from the stands. As in a haze Ken saw the long lines of white-sleeved students become violently agitated and move up and down to strange, crashing yells.

Then Ken Ward knew. That was the famed Place cheer for victory at the last stand. It was the trumpet call of Ken's ordeal. His mind was as full of flashes of thought as there were streaks and blurs before his eyes. He understood Worry now. He knew now what was wrong with him, what had been coming all through that terrible game. The whole line of stands and bleachers wavered before him, and the bright colors blended in one mottled band.

Still it was in him to fight to the last gasp. The pain in his breast, and the nausea in his stomach, and the whirling fury in his mind did not make him give up, though they robbed him of strength. The balls he threw to Prince were wide of the plate and had nothing of his old speed. Prince, also, took his base on balls.

Bases full and two out!

MacNeff, the captain, fronted the plate and shook his big bat at Ken. Of all the Place hitters Ken feared him the least. He had struck MacNeff out twice, and deep down in his heart stirred a last desperate rally. He had only to keep the ball high and in close to win this game. Oh! for the control that had been his pride!

The field and stands seemed to swim round Ken, and all he saw with his half-blinded eyes was the white plate, the batter, and Dean and the umpire. Then he took his windup and delivered the ball.

It went true. MacNeff missed it.

Ken pitched again. The umpire held up one

finger of each hand. One ball and one strike. Two more rapid pitches, one high and one wide. Two strikes and two balls.

Ken felt his head bursting and there were glints of red before his eyes. He bit his tongue to keep it from hanging out. He was almost done. That ceaseless, infernal din had benumbed his being. With a wrenching of his shoulder Ken flung up another ball. MacNeff leaned over it, then let it go by.

Three and two!

It was torture for Ken. He had the game in his hands, yet could not grasp it. He braced himself for the pitch and gave it all he had left in him.

"Too low!" he moaned. MacNeff killed low balls.

The big captain leaped forward with a terrific swing and hit the ball. It lined over short, then began to rise, shot over Homans, and soared far beyond, to drop and roll and roll.

Through darkening sight Ken Ward saw runner after runner score, and saw Homans pick up the ball as MacNeff crossed the plate with the winning run. In Ken's ears seemed a sound of the end of the world.

He thought himself the center of a flying wheel. It was the boys crowding around him. He saw their lips move but caught no words. Then choking and tottering, upheld by Reddy Ray's strong arm, the young pitcher walked off the field.

· 17 ·

KEN'S DAY

THE slow return to the tavern, dressing and going to the station, the ride home, the arrival at the training house, the close-pressing, silent companionship of Reddy Ray, Worry, and Raymond—these were dim details of that day of calamity. Ken Ward's mind was dead—locked on that fatal moment when he pitched a low ball to MacNeff. His friends left him in the darkness of his room, knowing instinctively that it was best for him to be alone.

Ken undressed and crawled wearily into bed and stretched out as if he knew and was glad he would never move his limbs again. The silence and the darkness seemed to hide him from himself. His mind was a whirling riot of fire, and in it was a lurid picture of that moment with MacNeff at bat. Over and over and over he lived it in helpless misery. His ears were muffled with that huge tide of sound. Again and again and again he pitched the last ball, to feel his heart stop beating, to see the big captain lunge at the ball, to watch it line and rise and soar.

But gradually exhaustion subdued his mental strife, and he wandered in mind and drifted into sleep. When he woke it was with a cold, unhappy shrinking from the day. His clock told the noon hour; he had slept long. Outside the June sunlight turned the maple leaves to gold. Was it possible, Ken wondered dully, for the sun ever to shine again? Then Scotty came bustling in.

"Mr. Wau-rd, won't ye be hovin' breakfast?" he asked anxiously.

"Scotty, I'll never eat again," replied Ken.

There were quick steps upon the stairs and Worry burst in, rustling a newspaper.

"Hello, old man!" he called cheerily. "Say! Look at this!"

He thrust the paper before Ken's eyes and pointed to a column:

Place Beat Wayne by a Lucky Drive. Young Ward
Pitched the Greatest Game Ever Pitched on Place
Field and Lost It in the Ninth, with Two
Men Out and Three and Two on MacNeff

Ken's dull, gloom-steeped mind underwent a change, but he could not speak. He sat up in bed, clutching the paper, and gazing from it to the coach. Raymond came in, followed by Homans, and, last, Reddy Ray, who sat down upon the bed.

They were all smiling, and that seemed horrible to Ken.

"But, Worry—Reddy—I—I lost the game— threw it away!" faltered Ken.

"Oh no, Peg. You pitched a grand game. Only in the stretch you got one ball too low," said Reddy.

"Peg, you started to go up early in the game," added Worry with a smile, as if the fact was amusing. "You made your first balloon ascension in the seventh. And in the ninth you exploded. I never seen a better case of up-in-the-air. But, Peg, in spite of it you pitched a wonderful game. You had me guessin'. I couldn't take you out of the box. Darn me if I didn't think you'd shut Place out in spite of your rattles!"

"Then—after all—it's not so terrible?" Ken asked breathlessly.

"Why, boy, it's all right. We can lose a game, and to lose one like that—it's as good as winnin'. Say! I'm a liar if I didn't see 'em Place hitters turnin' gray-headed! Listen! That game over there was tough on all the kids, you most of all, of course. But you all stood the gaff. You've fought out a grillin' big game away from home. That's over. You'll never go through that again. But it was the makin' of you. . . . Here, look this over! Mebbe it'll cheer you up."

He took something from Raymond and tossed it upon the bed. It looked like a round, red, woolly bundle. Ken unfolded it, to disclose a beautiful sweater, with a great white "W" in the center.

"The boys all got 'em this mornin'," added Worry.

It was then that the tragedy of the Place game lost its hold on Ken, and retreated until it stood only dimly in outline.

"I'll—I'll be down to lunch," said Ken irrelevantly.

His smiling friends took the hint and left the room.

Ken hugged the sweater while reading the *Times-Star*'s account of the game. Whoever the writer was, Ken loved him. Then he hid his face in the pillow, and though he denied to himself that he was crying, when he arose it was certain that the pillow was wet.

An hour later Ken presented himself at lunch, once more his old amiable self. The boys freely discussed baseball—in fact, for weeks they had breathed and dreamed baseball—but Ken noted, for the first time, where superiority was now added to the old confidence. The Wayne varsity had found itself. It outclassed Herne; it was faster than Place; it stood in line for championship honors.

"Peg, you needn't put on your uniform today," said the coach. "You rest up. But go over to Murray and have your arm rubbed. Is it sore or stiff?"

"Not at all. I could work again today," replied Ken.

That afternoon, alone in his room, he worked out his pitching plan for Saturday's game. It did not differ materially from former plans. But for a working basis he had self-acquired knowledge of the Place hitters. It had been purchased at dear cost. He feared none of them except Prince. He decided to use a high curveball over the plate and let Prince hit, trusting to luck and the players behind him. Ken remembered how the Place men had rapped hard balls at Raymond. Most of them were right-field hitters. Ken decided to ask Homans to play Reddy Ray in right field. Also he would arrange a sign with Reddy and Raymond and McCord so they would know when he intended to pitch a fastball on the outside corner of the plate. For both his curve and fastball so pitched were invariably hit toward right field. When it came to MacNeff, Ken knew from the hot rankling deep down in him that he would foil that hitter. He intended to make the others hit, pitching them always, to the best of his judgment and skill, those balls they were least likely to hit safely, yet which would cut the corners of the plate if let go. No bases on balls this game, that he vowed grimly. And if he got in a pinch he would fall back upon his last resort, the rising fastball; and now that he had gone through his baptism of fire he knew he was not likely to lose his control. So after outlining his plan he believed beyond reasonable doubt that he could win the game.

The evening of that day he confided his plan to Reddy Ray and had the gratification of hearing it warmly commended. While Ken was with Reddy the coach sent word up to all rooms that the boys were to "cut" baseball talk. They were to occupy their minds with reading, study, or games.

"It's pretty slow," said Reddy. "Peg, let's have some fun with somebody."

"I'm in. What'll we do?"

"Can't you think? You're always leaving schemes to me. Use your brains, boy."

Ken pondered a moment and then leaped up in great glee.

"Reddy, I've got something out of sight," he cried.

"Spring it, then."

"Well, it's this: Kel Raymond is perfectly crazy about his new sweater. He moons over it and he carries it around everywhere. Now it happens that Kel is a deep sleeper. He's hard to wake up. I've always had to shake him and kick him to wake him every morning. I'm sure we could get him in that sweater without waking him. So tomorrow morning you come down early, before seven, and help me put the sweater on Kel. We'll have Worry and the boys posted and we'll call them in to see Kel, and then we'll wake him and swear he slept in his sweater."

"Peg, you've a diabolical bent of mind. That'll be great. I'll be on the job bright and early."

Ken knew he could rely on the chattering of the sparrows in the woodbine around his window. They always woke him, and this morning was no exception. It was after six and a soft, balmy breeze blew in. Ken got up noiselessly and dressed. Raymond snored in blissful ignorance of the conspiracy. Presently a gentle tapping upon the door told Ken that Reddy was in the hall. Ken let him in and they held a whispered consultation.

"Let's see," said Reddy, picking up the sweater. "It's going to be an all-fired hard job. This sweater's tight. We'll wake him."

"Not on your life!" exclaimed Ken. "Not if we're quick. Now you roll up the sweater so—and stretch it on your hands—so—and when I lift Kel up you slip it over his head. It'll be like pie."

The operation was deftly though breathlessly performed, and all it brought from Raymond was a sleepy: "Aw—lemme sleep," and then he was gone again.

Ken and Reddy called all the boys, most of whom were in their pajamas, and Worry and Scotty and Murray, and got them all upstairs in

Raymond's room. Raymond lay in bed very innocently asleep, and no one would have suspected that he had not slept in his sweater.

"Well, I'll be doggoned!" ejaculated Worry, laughing till he cried. Murray was hugely delighted. These men were as much boys as the boys they trained.

The roar of laughter awakened Raymond, and he came out of sleep very languid and drowsy.

"Aw, Ken, lemme sleep s'more."

He opened his eyes and, seeing the room full of boys and men, he looked bewildered, then suspicious.

"Wull, what do all you guys want?"

"We only came in to see you asleep in your new varsity sweater," replied Ken, with charming candor.

At this Raymond discovered the sweater and he leaped out of bed.

"It's a lie! I never slept in it! Somebody tricked me! I'll lick him! . . . It's a lie, I say!"

He began to hop up and down in a black fury. The upper half of him was swathed in the red sweater; beneath that flapped the end of his short nightgown; and out of that stuck his thin legs, all knotted and spotted with honorable bruises won in fielding hard-batted balls. He made so ludicrous a sight that his visitors roared with laughter. Raymond threw books, shoes, everything he could lay his hands upon, and drove them out in confusion.

Saturday seemed a long time in arriving, but at last it came. All morning the boys kept close under cover of the training house. Someone sent them a package of placards. These were round, in the shape of baseballs. They were in the college colors, the background of which was a bright red, and across this had been printed in white the words: *"Peg Ward's Day!"*

"What do you think of that?" cried the boys with glistening eyes. But Ken was silent.

Worry came in for lunch and reported that the whole west end of the city had been placarded.

"The students have had millions of 'em cards printed," said Worry. "They're everywhere. Murray told me there was a hundred students tackin' 'em up on the stands and bleachers. They've got 'em on sticks of wood for pennants for the girls. . . . 'Peg Ward's Day!' Well, I guess!"

At two-thirty o'clock the varsity ran upon the field, to the welcoming though somewhat discordant music of the university band. What the music lacked in harmony it made up in volume, and as noise appeared to be the order of the day, it was most appropriate. However, a great booming cheer from the crowded stands drowned the band.

It was a bright summer day, with the warm air

swimming in the thick, golden light of June, with white clouds sailing across the blue sky. Grant Field resembled a beautiful crater with short, sloping sides of white and gold and great splashes of red and dots of black all encircling a round lake of emerald. Flashes of gray darted across the green, and these were the Place players in practice. Everywhere waved and twinkled and gleamed the red-and-white Wayne placards. And the front of the stands bore wide-reaching bands of these colored cards. The grandstand, with its pretty girls and gowns, and waving pennants, and dark-coated students, resembled a huge mosaic of many colors, moving and flashing in the sunlight. One stand set apart for the Place supporters was a solid mass of blue and gold. And opposite to it, in vivid contrast, was a long circle of bleachers, where five thousand red-placarded, red-ribboned Wayne students sat waiting to tear the air into shreds with cheers. Dale and Stevens and Bryan, wearing their varsity sweaters, strode to and fro on the cinder path, and each carried a megaphone. Cheers seemed to lurk in the very atmosphere. A soft, happy, subdued roar swept around the field. Fun and good nature and fair play and love of college pervaded that hum of many voices. Yet underneath it all lay a suppressed spirit, a hidden energy, waiting for the battle.

When Wayne had finished a brief, snappy practice, Kern, a National League umpire, called the game, with Place at bat. Ken Ward walked to the pitcher's slab amid a prolonged outburst, and ten thousand red cards bearing his name flashed like mirrors against the sunlight. Then the crashing Place yell replied in defiance.

Ken surveyed his fellow players, from whom came low, inspiriting words; then, facing the batter, Keene, he eyed him in cool speculation and swung into supple action.

The game started with a rush. Keene dumped the ball down the third-base line. Blake, anticipating the play, came rapidly in, and bending while in motion picked up the ball and made a perfect snap throw to McCord, beating Keene by a foot. Prince drove a hot grass-cutter through the infield, and the Place stand let out shrill, exultant yells. MacNeff swung powerfully on the first ball, which streaked like a flitting wing close under his chin. Prince, with a good lead, had darted for second. It was wonderful how his little, short legs carried him so swiftly. And his slide was what might have been expected of a famous football player. He hit the ground and shot into the bag just as Raymond got Dean's unerring throw too late. Again the Place rooters howled. MacNeff watched his second strike go by. The third pitch, remorselessly true to that fatal place, retired him on strikes; and a roll of thunder pealed from under the Wayne bleachers. Starke struck at the first ball given him. The Place waiters were not waiting on Ken today; evidently the word had gone out to hit. Ken's beautiful, speedy ball, chest high, was certainly a temptation. Starke lifted a long, lofty fly far beyond Homans, who ran and ran, and turned to get it gracefully at his chest.

Worry Arthurs sat stern and intent upon the Wayne bench. "Get that hit back and go them a run better!" was his sharp order.

The big, loose-jointed Salisbury, digging his foot into the dirt, settled down and swung laboriously. Homans waited. The pitch was a strike, and so was the next. But strikes were small matters for the patient Homans. He drew three balls after that, and then on the next he hit one of his short, punky safeties through the left side of the infield. The Wayne crowd accepted it with vigor of hands and feet. Raymond trotted up, aggressive and crafty. He intended to bunt, and the Place infield knew it and drew in closer. Raymond fouled one, then another, making two strikes. But he dumped the next and raced for the base. Salisbury, big and slow as he was, got the ball and threw Raymond out. Homans overran second, intending to go on, but, halted by Weir's hoarse coaching, he ran back.

When Reddy Ray stepped out it was to meet a rousing cheer, and then the thousands of feet went crash! crash! crash! Reddy fouled the first ball over the grandstand. Umpire Kern threw out a new one, gleaming white. The next two pitches were wide; the following one Reddy met with the short poke he used when hitting to left field. The ball went over Martin's head, scoring Homans with the first run of the game. That allowed the confident Wayne crowd to get up and yell long and loud. Weir fouled out upon the first ball pitched, and Blake, following him, forced Reddy out at second on an infield hit.

Place tied the score in the second inning on Weir's fumble of Martin's difficult grounder, a sacrifice by Horton, and Griffith's safe fly back of second.

With the score tied, the teams blanked inning after inning until the fifth. Wayne found Salisbury easy to bat against, but a Place player was always in front of the hit. And Place found Peg Ward unsolvable when hits meant runs. Ken kept up his tireless, swift cannonading over the plate, making his opponents hit, and when they got a runner on base he extended himself with the rising fastball. In the first of the fifth, with two out, Prince met one of Ken's straight ones hard and fair and drove the ball into the bleachers for a home run. That solid blue-and-gold square of Place supporters suddenly became an insane tossing, screeching mêlée.

The great hit also seemed to unleash the fiery spirit which had waited its chance. The Wayne players came in for their turn like angry bees.

Trace got a base on balls. Dean sacrificed. Ken also attempted to bunt and fouled himself out on strikes. Again Homans hit safely, but the crafty Keene, playing close, held Trace at third.

"We want the score!" Crash! crash! crash! went the bleachers.

With Raymond up and two out, the chance appeared slim, for he was not strong at batting. But he was great at trying, and this time, as luck would have it, he hit clean through second. Trace scored, and Homans, taking a desperate risk, tried to reach home on the hit and failed. It was fast, exciting work, and the crowd waxed hotter and hotter.

For Place the lumbering Horton hit a twisting grounder to McCord, who batted it down with his mitt, jumped for it, turned, and fell on the base, but too late to get his man. Griffith swung on Ken's straight ball and, quite by accident, blocked a little bunt out of reach of both Dean and Ken. It was a safe hit. Conroy stepped into Ken's fastball, which ticked his shirt, and the umpire sent him down to first amid the vociferous objections of the Wayne rooters.

Three runners on bases and no one out. How the Place students bawled and beat their seats and kicked the floor!

Ken took a longer moment of deliberation. He showed no sign that the critical situation unnerved him. But his supple shoulders knit closer, and his long arm whipped harder as he delivered the ball.

Salisbury, a poor batter, apparently shut his eyes and swung with all his might. All present heard the ringing crack of the bat, but few saw the ball. Raymond leaped lengthwise to the left and flashed out his glove. There was another crack, of a different sound. Then Raymond bounded over second base, kicking the bag, and with fiendish quickness sped the ball to first. Kern, the umpire, waved both arms wide. Then to the gasping audience the play became clear. Raymond had caught Salisbury's line drive in one hand, enabling him to make a triple play. A mighty shout shook the stands. Then strong, rhythmic, lusty cheers held the field in thrall for the moment, while the teams changed sides.

In Wayne's half of the sixth both Weir and McCord hit safely, but sharp fielding by Place held them on base.

Again the formidable head of Place's batting order was up. Keene lined to right field, a superb hit that looked good for a triple, but it did not have the speed to get beyond the fleet sprinter.

Ken eyed the curly-haired Prince as if he was saying to himself: "I'm putting them over today. Hit if you can!"

Prince appeared to jump up and chop Ken's first pitch. The ball struck on fair ground and bounded very high, and was a safe hit. Prince took a long lead off first base, and three times slid back to the bag when Ken tried to catch him. The fast football man intended to steal; Ken saw it, Dean saw it—everybody saw it. Whereupon Ken delivered a swift ball outside of the plate. As Prince went down little Dean caught the pitch and got the ball away quick as lightning. Raymond caught it directly in the baseline, and then, from the impact of the sliding Prince, he went hurtling down. Runner, baseman, and ball disappeared in a cloud of dust. Kern ran nimbly down the field and waved Prince off.

But Raymond did not get up. The umpire called time. Worry Arthurs ran out, and he and Weir carried Raymond to the bench, where they bathed his head and wiped the blood from his face.

Presently Raymond opened his eyes.

"Wull, what struck me?" he asked.

"Oh, nothin'. There was a trolley loose in the field," replied Worry. "Can you get up? Why did you try to block that football rusher?"

Raymond shook his head.

"Did I tag the big fat devil?" he queried, earnestly. "Is he out?"

"You got him a mile," replied Worry.

After a few moments Raymond was able to stand upon his feet, but he was so shaky that Worry sent Schoonover to second.

Then the cheering leaders before the bleachers

228

bellowed through their megaphones, and the students, rising to their feet, pealed out nine ringing "*Wayne!*"s and added a roaring "Raymond!" to the end.

With two out, Kern called for play.

Once again MacNeff was at bat. He had not made a foul in his two times up. He was at Ken's mercy, and the Wayne rooters were equally merciless.

"Ho! the slugging captain comes!"

"Get him a board!"

"Fluke hitter!"

"Mac, that was a lucky stab of yours Wednesday! Hit one *now!*"

No spectator of that game missed Ken's fierce impetuosity when he faced MacNeff. He was as keen-strung as a wire when he stood erect in the box, and when he got into motion he whirled far around, swung back bent, like a spring, and seemed to throw his whole body with the ball. One—two—three strikes that waved up in their velocity, and MacNeff for the third time went out.

Clatter and smash came from the bleachers, long stamping of feet, whistle and bang, for voices had become weak.

A hit, an error, a double play, another hit, a steal, and a force-out—these told of Wayne's dogged, unsuccessful trial for the winning run.

But Worry Arthurs had curtly said to his pitcher: "Peg, cut loose!" and man after man for

Place failed to do anything with his terrific speed. It was as if Ken had reserved himself wholly for the finish.

In the last of the eighth Dean hit one that caromed off Griffith's shin, and by hard running the little catcher made second. Ken sent him to third on a fielder's choice. It was then the run seemed forthcoming. Salisbury toiled in the box to coax the wary Homans. The Wayne captain waited until he got a ball to his liking. Martin trapped the hit and shot the ball home to catch Dean. It was another close decision, as Dean slid with the ball, but the umpire decided against the runner.

"Peg, hurl them over now!" called Reddy Ray.

It was the top of the ninth, with the weak end of Place's hitting strength to face Ken. Griffith, Conroy, Salisbury went down before him as grass before a scythe. To every hitter Ken seemed to bring more effort, more relentless purpose to baffle them, more wonderful speed and control of his fastball.

Through the stands and bleachers the word went freely that the game would go to ten innings, eleven innings, twelve innings, with the chances against the tiring Salisbury.

But on the Wayne bench there was a different order of conviction. Worry sparkled like flint. Homans, for once not phlegmatic, faced the coaching line at third. Raymond leaned pale and still against the bench. Ken was radiant.

Reddy Ray bent over the row of bats and singled out his own. His strong, freckled hands clenched the bat and whipped it through the air. His eyes were on fire when he looked at the stricken Raymond.

"Kel, something may happen yet before I get up to the plate," he said. "But if it doesn't—"

Then he strode out, knocked the dirt from his spikes, and stepped into position. Something about Reddy at that moment, or something potent in the unforeseen play to come, quieted the huge crowd.

Salisbury might have sensed it. He fussed with the ball and took a long while to pitch. Reddy's lithe form whirled around and seemed to get into running motion with the crack of the ball. Martin made a beautiful retrieval of the sharply bounding ball, but he might as well have saved himself the exertion. The championship sprinter beat the throw by yards.

Suddenly the whole Wayne contingent arose in a body, a tribute to what they expected of Reddy, and rent Grant Field with one tremendous outburst.

As it ceased a hoarse voice of stentorian volume rose and swelled on the air.

"*Wayne wins!* WATCH HIM RUN!"

It came from Murray, who loved his great sprinter.

Thrice Salisbury threw to MacNeff to hold

Reddy close to first base, but he only wasted his strength. Then he turned toward the batter, and he had scarcely twitched a muscle in the beginning of his swing, when the keen sprinter was gone like a flash. His running gave the impression of something demonlike forced by the wind. He had covered the ground and was standing on the bag when Prince caught Conroy's throw.

Pandemonium broke out in the stands and bleachers, and a piercing, continuous scream. The sprinter could not be stopped. That was plain. He crouched low, watching Salisbury. Again and again the pitcher tried to keep Reddy near second base, but as soon as Martin or Prince returned the ball Reddy took his lead off the bag. He meant to run on the first pitch; he was on his toes. And the audience went wild, and the Place varsity showed a hurried, nervous strain. They yelled to Salisbury, but neither he nor anyone else could have heard a thunderbolt in that moment.

Again Salisbury toed the rubber, and he hesitated, with his face turned toward second. But he had to pitch the ball, and as his elbow trembled the sprinter shot out of his tracks with the start that had made him famous. His red hair streaked in the wind like a waving flame. His beautiful stride swallowed distance. Then he sailed low and slid into the base as the ball struck Griffith's hands.

Reddy was on third now, with no one out, with

two balls upon Weir and no strikes. In the fury of sound runner and batter exchanged a glance that was a sign.

The sprinter crouched low, watching Salisbury. For the third time, as the pitcher vibrated with the nervous force preceding his delivery, Reddy got his start. He was actually running before the ball left Salisbury's hand. Almost it seemed that with his marvelous fleetness he was beating the ball to the plate. But as the watchers choked in agony of suspense Weir bunted the ball, and Reddy Ray flashed across the plate with the winning run.

Then all that seemed cheering, din, and stamping roar deadened in an earthshaking sound like an avalanche.

The students piled out of the bleachers in streams and poured on the field. An irresistible, hungry, clamoring flood, they submerged the players.

Up went Ken upon sturdy shoulders, and up went Reddy Ray and Kel and Homans and Dean—all the team, and last the red-faced Worry Arthurs. Then began the triumphant march about Grant Field and to the training house.

It was a Wayne day, a day for the varsity, for Homans and Raymond, and for the great sprinter, but most of all it was Peg Ward's day.

· 18 ·

BREAKING TRAINING

THE Wayne varsity was a much-handled, storm-tossed team before it finally escaped the clutches of the students. Every player had a ringing in his ears and a swelling in his heart. When the baseball uniforms came off they were carefully packed in the bottoms of trunks, and twelve varsity sweaters received as tender care as if they were the flimsy finery dear to the boys' sisters.

At six the players were assembled in the big reading room, and there was a babel of exultant conversation. Worry suddenly came in, shouting to persons without who manifestly wanted to enter. "Nothin' doin' yet! I'll turn the boys over to you in one hour!" Then he banged the door and locked it.

Worry was a sight to behold. His collar was unbuttoned, and his necktie disarranged. He had no hat. His hair was damp and rumpled, and his red face worked spasmodically.

"Where's Peg?" he yelled, and his little bright

eyes blinked at his players. It was plain that Worry could not see very well then. Someone pushed Ken out, and Worry fell on his neck. He hugged him close and hard. Then he dived at Reddy and mauled him. Next he fell all over little crippled Raymond, who sat propped up in an armchair. For once Raymond never murmured for being jumped on. Upon every player, and even the substitutes, Worry expressed his joy in violent manner, and then he fell down himself, perspiring, beaming, utterly exhausted. This man was not the cold, caustic coach of the cage days, nor the stern, hard ruler from the bench, nor the smooth worker on his players' feelings. This was Worry Arthurs with his varsity at the close of a championship season. No one but the boys who had fought at his bidding for Wayne ever saw him like that.

"Oh, Peg, it was glorious! This game gives us the record and the championship. Say, Peg, this was the great game for you to win. For you made Place hit, and then when they got runners on bases you shut down on 'em. You made MacNeff look like a dud. You gave that home run to Prince."

"I sure was after MacNeff's scalp," replied Ken. "And I put the ball over for Prince to hit. What else could I do? Why, that little chunky cuss has an eye, and he can sting the ball—he's almost as good as Reddy. But, Worry, you mustn't give me the credit. Reddy won the game, you know."

"You talk like a kid," replied Reddy, for once not cool and easy. "I cut loose and ran some; but, Peg, you and Raymond won the game."

"Wull, you make me sick," retorted Raymond, threatening to get up. "There wasn't anything to this day but Peg Ward."

Ken replied with more heat than dignity, and quick as a flash he and Reddy and Raymond were involved in a wordy war, trying to place the credit for winning the game. They dragged some of the other boys into the fierce argument.

Worry laughed and laughed; then, as this loyal bunch of players threatened to come to blows, he got angry.

"*Shut up!*" he roared. "I never seen such a lot of hot-headed kids. Shut up, and let me tell you who won this Place game. It'll go down on record as a famous game, so you'll do well to have it straight. Listen! The Wayne varsity won this game. Homans, your captain, won it, because he directed the team and followed orders. He hit and ran some, too. Reddy Ray won this game by bein' a blue streak of chain lightnin' on the bases. Raymond won it by makin' a hit when we all expected him to fall dead. He won it twice, the second time with the greatest fieldin' play ever pulled off on Grant Field. Dean won the game by goin' up and hangin' onto Peg's rising fastball. McCord won it by diggin' low throws out of the dirt. Weir was around when it happened, wasn't he—and Blake and Trace? Then there was Peg himself. He won the game a *little*. Say! he had Place trimmed when he stepped on the slab in the first innin'. So you all won the big Wayne–Place game."

Then Worry advanced impressively to the table, put his hand in his breast pocket, and brought forth a paper.

"You've won this for me, boys," he said, spreading the paper out.

"What is it?" they asked wonderingly.

"Nothin' of much importance to you boys as compared with winnin' the game, but some to Worry Arthurs." He paused with a little choke. "It's a five-year contract to coach Wayne's baseball teams."

A thundering cheer attested to the importance of that document to the boys.

"Oh, Worry, but I'm glad!" cried Ken. "Then your son Harry will be in college next year—will he be on the team?"

"Say, he'll have to go some to make next year's varsity, with only two or three vacancies to fill. Now, fellows, I want to know things. Sit down now and listen."

They all took seats, leaving the coach standing at the table.

"Homans, is there any hope of your comin' back to college next year?"

"None, I'm sorry to say," replied the captain.

"Father intends to put me in charge of his business."

"Reddy, how about a postgraduate course for you? You need that P.G."

"Worry, come to think of it, I really believe my college education would not be complete without that P.G.," replied Reddy, with the old cool speech and a merry twinkle in his eye.

At this the boys howled like Indians, and Worry himself did a little war dance.

"Raymond, you'll come back?" went on the coach.

The second baseman appeared highly insulted. "Come back? Wull, what do you take me for? I'd like to see the guy who can beat me out of my place next season."

This brought another hearty cheer.

Further questioning made clear that all the varsity except Homans, Blake, and McCord would surely return to college.

"Fine! Fine! Fine!" exclaimed Worry.

Then he began to question each player as to what he intended to do through the summer months, and asked him to promise not to play ball on any summer squads.

"Peg, you're the one I'm scared about," said Worry earnestly. "These crack teams at the seashore and in the mountains will be hot after you. They've got coin too, Peg, and they'll spend it to get you."

"All I've got to say is they'll waste their breath talking to me," replied Ken with a short laugh.

"What are you goin' to do all summer?" asked Worry curiously. "Where will you be?"

"I expect to go to Arizona."

"Arizona? What in the deuce are you goin' way out there for?"

Ken paused and then, when he was about to reply, Raymond burst out:

"Worry, he says it's forestry, but he only took up that fool subject because he likes to chase around in the woods. He's nutty about trees and bears and mustangs. He was in Arizona last summer. You ought to hear some of the stories he's told me. Why, if they're true he's got Frank Nelson and Jim Hawkins skinned to a frazzle."

"For instance?" asked Worry, very much surprised and interested.

"Why, stories about how he was chased and captured by outlaws, and lassoed bears, and had scraps with Mexicans, and was in wild caves and forest fires, and lots about a Texas ranger who always carried two big guns. I've had the nightmare ever since we've been in the training house. Oh, Ken can tell stories, all right. He's as much imagination as he's got speed with a ball. And say, Worry, he's got the nerve to tell me that this summer he expects to help an old hunter lasso mountain lions out there in Arizona. What do you think of that?"

"It's straight goods!" protested Ken, solemnly facing the bright-eyed boys.

"We want to go along!" yelled everybody.

"Say, Peg, I ain't stuck on that idee, not a little bit," replied the coach dubiously.

"Worry has begun to worry about next season. He's afraid Peg will get that arm chewed off," put in Reddy.

"Well, if I've got to choose between lettin' Peg chase mountain lions and seein' him chased by 'em fathead directors, I'll take my chances with the lions."

Then all in a moment Worry became serious.

"Boys, it's time to break trainin'. I ain't got much to say. You're the best team I ever developed. Let it go at that. In a few minutes you are free to go out to the banquets and receptions, to all that's waitin' for you. And it will be great. Tomorrow you will be sayin' good-bye to me and to each other and scatterin' to your homes. But let's not forget each other and how we plugged this year. Sure, it was only baseball, but, after all, I think good, hard play, on the square and against long odds, will do as much for you as your studies. Let the old baseball coach assure you of that."

He paused, paced a few steps to and fro, hands behind his back, thoughtful and somewhat sad.

The members of the varsity sat pale and still, faces straight before them, eyes shining with memory of that long uphill struggle, and glistening, too, with the thought that the time had come for parting.

"Homans, will you please see to the election of the new captain?" said Worry.

Homans stepped out briskly and placed a hat, twelve folded slips of paper, and a pencil upon the table.

"Fellows, you will follow me in our regular batting order," directed Homans. "Each man is to write his name on one side of a slip of paper and his choice for captain on the other side. Drop the paper in the hat."

Homans seated himself at the table and quickly cast his vote. Raymond hobbled up next. Reddy Ray followed him. And so, in silence, and with a certain grave dignity of manner that had yet a suggestion of pleasure, the members of the varsity voted.

When they had resumed their seats Homans turned the slips out of the hat and unfolded them.

"These votes will be given to the athletic directors and kept on record," he said. "But we will never see but one side of them. That is Wayne's rule in electing captains, so the players will not know how each voted. But this is an occasion I am happy to see when we shall all know who voted for who. It shall be a little secret of which we will never speak."

He paused while he arranged the slips neatly together.

"There are here twelve votes. Eleven have been cast for one player—one for another player! Will you all please step forward and look?"

In an intense stillness the varsity surrounded the table. There was a sudden sharp gasp from one of them.

With a frank, glad smile Homans held out his hand.

"CAPTAIN WARD!"